MORE

than our

BLUES

Unfettered Expressions from Confined Persons

COMMUNITY
EDUCATION
PROJECT

Editor: Denise Lussier Yezbick
Assistant Editor: Carley Fockler
Book Designer/Publication Consultant: Lucianna Chixaro Ramos
Cover Art: Chris & Patrick
Cover Design: Lucianna Chixaro Ramos

Printed in the United States of America

First Printing, 2020

ISBN 978-1-7344242-0-1

Community Education Project
Stetson University
Elizabeth Hall #207
421 N. Woodland Blvd. Unit 8325
DeLand, Florida 32723

MORE

than our

BLUE$

Unfettered Expressions from Confined Persons

CONTENTS

INTRODUCTION

Community Education Project is a higher education in prison program run by faculty from Stetson University. Established in 2015, CEP offers for-credit college-level courses and other educational programs to incarcerated individuals at Tomoka Correctional Institution, in Daytona Beach. CEP's mission is to provide quality liberal arts education in Florida prisons. With that in mind the CEP team, volunteers, and students have worked together to develop numerous educational initiatives to promote meaningful opportunities for personal growth and intellectual engagement to all participants as well as to build communities inside and outside prison.

More Than Our Blues, an anthology of student creative writing, has grown out of one of those signature initiatives focused on college writing and creative and critical thinking through lecture series and writing-intensive courses. Although CEP students have been writing well before joining the program, the idea for this first in-house publication came about in 2018 after CEP students completed a workshop on poetry led by Dr. Denise Yezbick, which culminated with students performing their own work in front of the class. Thanks to the passion and dedication of all CEP students, leadership of Dr. Yezbick and assistant editor Carley Fockler as well as generous financial support from the Nina B. Hollis Institute for Educational Reform at Stetson University, what started as an idea, is now a rich collection of poems, short stories, autobiographical narratives, and thought-provoking reflections on life, resilience, voice, personhood, hope, family, memories, and daily life inside and outside prison written by current and former CEP students.

This publication would also not be possible without the financial support of Laughing Gull Foundation as well as the time, energy, skills, knowledge, and experience of numerous volunteers, Stetson colleagues, and student interns who have been supporting CEP since its inception.

—Dr. Jelena Petrovic

Storytelling is fundamentally human. Sharing experiences and communicating feelings is within each of us. This collection shows that more clearly than most. These students have experiences and voices that are so often limited, quieted, or ignored despite the fact that their stories are so relevant and engaging.

I joined this project after it had started, but quickly found myself doing more than editing. Through their writing, these students reinforced the value of being heard and storytelling. Because of the willingness of these students to offer connections, experiences, and engaging memories – I felt that I understood not only these individuals, but the world better.

These authors show that no physical barrier, no label, and no societal limitation can hinder the connection between people. They share pieces with themes that all can relate to: exploring the self, finding meaning in life, struggling with hope, coping with major life changes, and existing as a human.

Perhaps the most prevalent and powerful element of this collection is the way it lingers. These stories are still with me, making me question much of what I originally accepted as fact.

This book will showcase the work of very talented and driven authors and lead the readers to reframe their thoughts about society, connection, and the human spirit.

—*Carley Fockler*

A few years ago I came in contact with Community Education Project. After teaching a few literature courses to the men in the program, their love for not only reading literature but for writing became apparent to me. A class that started out studying poetry ended with the students sharing their own.

Thus, the idea of this journal came into being. Many months and revisions later you now hold it in your hands. A physical copy of the thoughts and imaginings of a handful of men whose life experiences have led them on paths that most of us never have to consider.

You may notice from some of the titles of the selections in this book that they are a piece of a much larger, or an ongoing writing project. Many of these students are prolific authors who were writing long before CEP professors and volunteers came in contact with them. Others have discovered more recently that writing is an outlet for expression that they love, as well as a tool to process their thoughts. All of them have written their truths, whether fiction, non-fiction, or poetry.

Working on this project has been a rich experience, sometimes accomplished from afar through digital transmissions with the daily visiting professor, and other times through face to face sessions with the students. It has not been without its challenges due to the circumstances of their confinement, but through it all, collaborating with these men has been gratifying and productive.

Through writing, they express a freedom they still maintain—freedom of thought. When I read these selections, I experience many emotions; I am taken by the honesty and rawness of experience, the beauty of the language, the hope and despair of the narrators. This book is to be enjoyed, but may it also cause us to consider how the words and thoughts expressed relate to us in the society we inhabit.

This introduction is not complete without hearing from the students in CEP. This project is of their making from the cover design, the title, and, of course, the contents. Different ones of them participated in this project in different ways, but it has been guided by CEP's pedagogical approach, best described by Alex in the program:

"On January 16, 2015, three professors from Stetson University (Andy Eisen, Pamela Cappas-Toros, and Jelena Petrovic) came into Tomoka Correctional Institution (TCI) with a plan to bring higher education to the Florida Department of Corrections. Along with that plan, they brought a compassion to teach and the determination to see their plan through . . .They taught in a way that also empowered us to teach ourselves, and at the same time allowed themselves to learn from us."

As someone who began as a non-Stetson volunteer in the program, I have always been struck by the respect afforded everyone involved in the program as well as the dialectical approach between teachers and students.

—*Dr. Denise Lussier Yezbick*

FROM THE AUTHORS

"The act of writing is very important to me because when I got locked up I was functionally illiterate. Being able to communicate effectively with others is critical. [Writing] demonstrates that there are a lot of good people in prison. These people may have been products of their environments or they just made a mistake. To represent men and women who are incarcerated by my involvement in this project makes me very humbled and honored."

—Greg

"To me, writing is an art of clarifying thoughts and expanding ideas. It is also a therapeutic undertaking: by recapturing a moment of time, an emotion, it cleanses my mind and heart, and allows me to see the moment with the benefit of hindsight. Moreover, with that hindsight, I can engage others and perhaps help them navigate similar difficult circumstances.

Everyone, generally, has their reasons for the things they have done or do. Some of those reasons are flawed, but they are human reasons. Humans are flawed. They are unique, and in the end, everyone wants to be understood. My words are my way of conveying my grief, frustration, hope, and love, and to connect with my fellow men and women."

—Roger

"The act of writing is the essence of transmuting thoughts into a more bodily form, a step to giving life to ideas. Writing gives me a chance to give matter to my thoughts, feelings, and perceptions. This publication gives me a sense of accomplishment, and a sense of being involved in a matter that has purpose, which is a gift in the circumstances that I am currently in."

—*Niko*

"I am happy to share my private thoughts with readers outside of these fences. As a person condemned to social death for the rest of his life, I am thrilled by the prospect of my thoughts and feelings inspiring others to reflect on the dangers of reducing complex human beings with labels like 'inmate,' 'convict,' and 'murderer.' I feel that by contributing to this publication I am challenging powerful penological and political discourses that deny the essential humanity of countless men, women, and children who move through a harsh criminal justice system."

—*Antonio*

"The act of writing is a cathartic release of the many things I have been forced to repress over the decades. I have many stories to tell, but no one to share them with. MTOB has given me a voice! This book will also be an avenue for my estranged family to remotely reconnect and maybe see me in the light of today rather than that of three decades ago.

I must keep so much inside, so many secrets. There are some things that can be shared, but only in the right environment, or through the right outlet, and still be safe for me to do so. However, there are some that must go to my grave. The mere act of saying actually relieves some of the pressures that have built up in me like a head of steam in the old boiler I used to operate. I also feel that so much of what Hollywood has shown of prison life has skewed the public's perception of us [in prison]. This is an opportunity to allow the American public and the English reading world to know our truths."

—Michael

"Writing allows me the time to occupy myself with a positive activity while I am incarcerated. My wishes are that the reader appreciates us collectively as more than just prisoners or criminals who some believe deserve only punishment.

Writing actually changed who I am. It allowed me to increase my vocabulary, my thinking. I come from an impoverished location and creative writing projects are rare to non-existent. My family was shocked when I informed them that I am co-authoring a book with my fellow Stetson students. To know that the world will have an opportunity to see that I am more than just the crime and the uniform I currently wear, will bring a sense of relief. I've discovered there is power in writing."

—Ben

"The act of writing is my freedom of expression of my thought process and an art that can reach people without requiring a physical presence. [MTOB] allows me to realize, despite our current state of incarceration, our voice and ideas are still relevant. Writing has become more therapeutic and a form of self-medication assisting me to take positive and negative emotions and turn those emotions into art."

—Robert

"Writing is an outlet for my feelings, a means to express myself. [It has opened] my eyes to my surroundings in ways that would not have been in the forefront of my mind before."

—*Earl*

"Never before have I written creatively where the work is scrutinized and worked over as if I was a published author. Not only has this allowed me to have a voice to speak the feelings that run through my life, but it has also brought validity to my ideas and personal reflections.

Having my work reviewed and deemed worthy of being viewed makes me feel as if my inner thoughts and feelings need to be shared with others and be given a voice. In prison, expression is curtailed; you don't want to offend other people or bring unwanted attention to yourself. Allowing me to write, given where I am at, reminds me that there is a life and lifestyle outside of what I am experiencing at the current moment. For that I am grateful."

—*Jacob*

"This year has been a tremendous year of loss for my family. This project gave me an outlet to be creative instead of being overcome by self-destructive grief. I know my works are not going to appeal to everyone, but it is MY work and that is all that truly matters."

—*David*

blue(s)

\ blü \ — *noun*

> blueness (resembling the color of the clear sky in the daytime); blue sky, wild blue yonder

\ blü \ — *adjective*

> of the color intermediate between green and violet; gloomy, grim, depressed, dispirited, down, downcast, downhearted, down in the mouth, low, low-spirited

\ blü \ — *verb*

> turn blue

THE DIFFERENCE IN WEIGHT

John W.

It wasn't such an unpleasant job, as far as prison job assignments go. Troy had been a confinement orderly for a bit more than a week now; it even seemed like it could be somewhat nice. He had to get up at 3:30 am to be there in time to pass out breakfast at 4:30 a.m., but he was still grateful it kept him out of the kitchen. Those guys had to get up at 3 a.m. and they stayed until 11 a.m.; Troy was out of there every day at 6 am. Not only that, but all he had to do was handle the breakfast cart and a little sweeping and mopping – no sweat.

Some of the officers would even let him hustle. Like the officer he was working with now, Officer Moody. Moody seemed alright. Now that Troy had worked there a few days, he knew which cops would actually strip search him coming in and out and which shifts would merely pretend; Moody didn't even make him take off his blues. Troy could traffic all sorts of stuff past Moody; the officer didn't care at all. Just today, he had brought in two bars of soap, three packs of batteries, and a few Reader's Digest magazines. He was going to be leaving with at least five books of stamps – the profit from the soap and batteries.

With Moody, he could also hustle trays. Extra trays went for five stamps each, and Moody didn't care if he sold the cart itself, along with the contents. In fact, yesterday, Troy had messed up and sold too many trays. Moody had to call Food Service and order more so they could finish the last of wing 3. Moody was sweet.

"Air-tray this asshole," Moody told him now.

"Sir?" Troy was startled.

Moody stood there, held the tray flap open, and watched him with an empty expression. Did Troy hear him right? Officer Moody looked directly into Troy's eyes and said with serene clarity, "Air. Tray. Him."

Troy had heard about this sort of thing in the county jail. An air-tray was exactly what it sounded like – a tray of air, empty. It appeared legitimate for the hallway camera, so the guy behind the door couldn't file a grievance claiming that he hadn't been fed; he would have a hungry, miserable day.

Troy was frozen. He didn't want to do it. It wasn't that he was worried the guy behind the door might catch up with him out on the compound. Troy didn't want to do it because he knew it wasn't right. It was fundamentally different than breaking any rule. Prison rules are oppressive; they are meant to be broken, however, Troy had been raised to do unto others as he would have them do unto him. He couldn't imagine having to spend a hungry day in the box himself. Troy didn't have to do it either; he could just as easily reach for the next full tray as he could the empty one. What could Moody do, beat Troy up? Lie, and give him a false disciplinary report? He couldn't imagine either; of these things, not from Moody. Troy liked Moody; Moody let him hustle.

Troy glanced over at the cell window, but couldn't see the face of the man behind the door. He could see his shadow on the cell wall, but not his face. Troy was hoping that knowing who it was would help him to explain that he couldn't do it, but he couldn't imagine why the identity of the man would matter. Troy was only casting his gaze about, searching for a way out of the trap he'd fallen into.

Moody cleared his throat expectantly. Even as Troy was trying to think of a way to explain to Moody that he couldn't do it, Troy's hands moved on their own accord in defiance of the signals his brain was sending. Numerous scenarios ran through his mind, but they got all tangled up against each other; he couldn't sort them into a plan.

Troy believed that he was going to make a stand; he envisioned himself telling officer Moody he was sorry, that he couldn't do it. He envisioned himself picking up the full tray, in defiance of officer Moody, and handing it through the flap. He saw, in his mind, the disappointed look Moody would have on his face, felt the weight of the knowledge that Troy's relationship with Moody would forever change. Troy tested his willingness to bear the repercussions of defying Officer Moody. He imagined that knowledge of imminent ramifications, and he believed he could do what he knew to be right, despite the consequences.

He believed it until the guy behind the door took the empty tray from Troy's traitorous hands.

The hungry man expected a full, heavy tray, but the reality was hollow. The difference in weight between expectation and reality caused him to bang the tray against the top of the door's flap.

"Bonk," said the empty tray. To Troy, it was an accusation, a condemnation.

Just before moving on to the next cell, Troy's eyes moved from the flap to the cell window. He only saw his own reflection in the glass. The florescent lights made him look flat and empty; the mottled and thick glass made him appear distorted – slightly grotesque.

AN AVERAGE DAY

Jacob

He sits at his usual chair, the one closest to the electrical outlet. Too far and he won't be able to reach. Luckily for him, like most days, the chair was available for his posterior. *As it should be,* he thinks, *they all know I like to set up near the outlet.*

Sitting, he makes his usual greetings. The greetings are returned; a follow up question is posed, a unique change from the routine. "Shouldn't you be in class now?"

Class? As if you could call that a class. Expecting individuals to sit through an impersonal and unenlightening lecture does not constitute a class. Especially when one is only echoing the current week's readings. Although someone may be adept enough to stagger through a doctoral program, it must obviously not equate to being an interactive person.

"Decided to skip it; needed a break." He produces the laptop from his backpack and constructs his usual setup: laptop three inches from the lip of the table, mousepad and mouse at a respectable distance to the right, and the power cord trailing on the left to the outlet. The last thing he needs is for wires to cross.

Situated as well as he can be on hard plastic, he opens the laptop and starts it up. The others around the table have gone back to their own conversations, laptops, or phones. A crumpled bag from the food court restaurant, Moe's, lies near an occupant's area. Typical for a Monday.

He roams through the Internet, checking to see if there are

any updates to the slew of social media that he has but doesn't post one. He sees that the Internet has produced its generic daily content: an article detailing a new medical discovery, probably something to do with a controversial diet, an argument by someone professing the injustices of the government, and a picture of a cat. Always a cat. It's as if the world, at least those that dwell on the Internet, have become fascinated with all things feline.

Maybe that's why my roommates got the cat for the apartment, he ponders. There sure were a lot of people who like to post about their cats. Maybe they were going to join the rest of the world in displaying their feline on the Internet. If they ended up creating a Facebook profile for the thing, he'd approach them concerning the subject.

Satisfied that he has kept current with the latest in cat dress-ups, he allows his concentration to drift. He lingers on conversations others at the table are having concerning events of the past weekend. Apparently several of them had gone to an event, something to do with the beach. Sounds like fun. What did he do this weekend? If asked, he'd reframe the question: what didn't he do? At least that list would be longer.

It wasn't his fault that his weekend lacked an exciting tale. The roommates had been out all weekend doing their own activities, leaving him alone with the cat. The rest of the people at the table knew how to get ahold of him if they required his inclusion.

Besides, it had been an eventful weekend. He'd wrapped up season 5 of *How I Met Your Mother*, sitting in his bed with the laptop held on his lap while he reveled in the comedy and ultimate destiny-induced completion of true love. And it hadn't been all monotony. He'd taken breaks from the show to socially interact through League of Legends. That had to count for something, right? It wasn't like he was aimlessly wasting his time. Besides, he had progressed towards his goal of increasing his win percentage to over fifty-five. In fact, after class tonight he would go back to his apartment and play some more. Maybe he'd be able to finally win enough matches to advance to the next tiered bracket.

"Have you had lunch yet?" Broken from his thoughts, he notices the new arrival seated next to him.

"No," he says. There hadn't been anything to eat in the apartment and he hadn't felt up to the task of grocery shopping. Too much of a hassle deciding what would be cooked, making the trip to the store, buying the goods, fighting for space to put it in the shared refrigerator. Then there was the actual issue of cooking. It isn't that he didn't like to cook, that was always the easiest part. It was the cleaning. If he waited too long to clean up, his roommates would get mad; if he cleaned up immediately, it would be like he had never been there.

His roommates never understood this. Everything had to be clean, put away, nice and ordered. As if no one ate or inhabited the area. No mark, no trail. No sign of existence. All for the sake of cleanliness. It made sense to them, but not to him. The whole point of having your own living space was to have it be lived in. So what if a plate remained in the sink for an hour or two while he did something else? The world wasn't going to end if the place was a little cluttered. But that's how they wanted the kitchen to be, so he left it like that; better yet he avoided the area all together.

"Go get some Moe's so I can have some chips," the new arrival insists of him as she stands, brokering no room for discussion. He is hungry and it was Monday after all. Moe's was always cheaper on Mondays, and besides, if he was going to be skipping class he might as well indulge in all-you-can-eat chips—another thing he had learned from his voyages on the Internet, and something that had brought him fame and acclaim when he had announced it to the other occupants at the table weeks prior. After verifying the truth of the claim, the table had been littered with bags from Moe's for the rest of the day. He had been hailed a hero.

"Sure." He extracts himself from his setup, and makes the short walk towards the food court with the girl. She doesn't order anything for herself, though she stays with him while he waits in line for his turn at the counter. She berates him upon learning that he is skipping class, though forgets that as soon as he hands her the bag filled with chips. She has what she wants, and she's satisfied for now. He, on the other hand, has acquired his usual order: a chicken burrito, extra meat, no rice, pinto beans, salsa, sour cream, cheese, and enough bacon to make a cardiologist blush. Didn't even have to ask the worker to mix all the ingredients before wrapping it in the burrito. He has been here enough times to become familiar to the workers, and they know how he likes his meal.

They make their way back to the table, the girl not even waiting for the food to be paid at the register before she begins digging into the chips. *They say that everything free tastes better*, he thinks, as he sits at his chair and moves the laptop out of the way. That's another thing to avoid with the laptop—food particles getting between the keys. Once they get in, they require complete removal of the keys to get clean. He doesn't want to clean, so the laptop is moved aside to make room for his burrito.

He eats while the girl shares her chips with others and makes conversation. She's regaling them with tales of her class that morning, the one where she goes to local elementary schools and sits in while she learns how to become a teacher. Student teaching, she animatedly calls it, telling the story with her hands as much as with her words. There's no doubt in her mind that she wants to become a teacher. Even the smallest thing, such as to-day's tale of a small child asking her how to pronounce her name, brings delight to her day.

The delight of his day? The burrito answers that question for him, though soon enough that is gone and he's left in the same position that he was before. He moves the trash aside and resumes his setup from before, cutting off the girl as she begins another tale. Apparently she gets to lead the children through a science experiment tomorrow. He doesn't hear the rest as he puts his headphones back in. Just as well, or he'd have to sit through more stories of how much fun it is to be a teacher.

He allows for his music to play, drowning out the noise that surrounds him, and busies himself with his constant vigilance of the Internet, though he knows there won't be anything substantially new since the last time he checked. Still, it won't hurt to look; it's not like he has anything else to do, which he knows isn't true. He still has a paper due for his class that night, a paper that he hasn't even begun to write. But that's what makes it exciting. If he would finish it in time and get a good grade, then he would be able to justify his inactivity for the past weekend.

Sighing, he decides to work on his paper.

But what to write about? His professor told him it needs to be a creative piece. With such broad criteria he should be able to figure out what to write about. Then again, he's not in a creative mood. If anybody has creativity, it is the girl next to him, and she seems to be sucking all the creativity from the space. Just now, as he glances up to take a look, she has everyone enthralled by her stories. They're laughing, probably at something else that a small child told her today.

Sighing again, he stares back at his laptop still showing the same cat photo that had been reposted several times over the past week. 'I had fun once. It was terrible,' is captioned over the face of the very grumpy looking cat. Maybe I should write about this, he thinks. How cats have taken over as a way to express human emotions. He could even talk about how his roommates had gotten sucked into this psychological conundrum with their purchase of a feline.

Instead, he begins to browse through the vastness of the Internet attempting to find some non-feline inspiration for his work. There's not much to find though; his searches send him back to his usual results: video games, jokes only people who spent their free time on the Internet would get, and porn. He wonders how the innocent search of creative pieces led him to porn, but then he remembers the rare instance when his roommates had barged into his room to show him something that they had found on the Internet. Apparently, there were things that even he had never seen, and things that he never wanted to see once they had finished showing him the first video. It did answer the unsought question of what amputee people do for fun, not that he could ever use such information as an ice breaker. "Hey, have you ever thought about how people without limbs pleasure their partner?" It is better to avoid such controversial topics, he thinks, moving on through his selection of results.

He feels a tap on his shoulder that breaks his concentration. He lifts his headphones and sees that the girl has apparently finished her anthology to the other people at the table and they've all gone back to their respective tasks.

"What are you doing?" she inquires. When he explains the deadline for the paper she admonishes him for not doing his work earlier. "And you're skipping class too," she exclaims. "Don't you ever get work done?"

"I do," he says. *I don't*, he thinks.

"You also need to get your work done so you can go to the basketball game this afternoon. Pep Band has to be there by three."

He reminds her, however, that he hadn't joined Pep Band this semester. He had been too busy to find time to go and play music at basketball games. In reality, he hadn't felt like signing on for something that wasn't required of him. Although the people at the table had enticed him with the idea of fun and, most importantly, the free trip they all got to take when the basketball team went to playoffs, he hadn't bothered. His lack of attendance doesn't seem to register with her or with the several other people at the table who have mild reactions when learning, again, that he hadn't joined the rest of them for Pep Band.

"Well that's good then. You'll have more time to finish your work," she tells him. He agrees as they all begin to depart, leaving him at the table, the Moe's bag left open, its insides excavated.

Alone at the table, he resumes his search for an idea for his paper. Nothing's working though. It seems that the Internet won't be saving him today.

Just as he's closing down his search, he notices a new post from the girl. She and the others have arrived at the basketball game, and she's posted a picture of their gathering. He sees the smiles they all have, arms wrapped around one another. Someone has already commented on the photo, exclaiming how much fun they're having with everyone at the game. It wasn't enough that they were there at the game, but they had to go and tell everyone what they were doing. The redundancy of it all.

And what does he have to show for his time? A blank paper and a due date that was ticking closer and closer. But he didn't feel like writing, finding himself staring at the image in front of him. Why hadn't he joined Pep band? He scrolls through images on the girl's photo album and stops on one dated less than a year ago.

In the picture, he stands with those who had previously occupied the table with him, striking a pose similar to the one they had just posed for at the basketball game. The only difference was that this one included him.

The image stares at him, bringing his mind back to months past when he thought, hoped, that the feelings he was experiencing would last forever. They hadn't even lasted the week.

Maybe it was all fake. Maybe it had been real at the time. Either way, he isn't involved now. It hadn't been for lack of want, or maybe it had been. He doesn't know anymore.

He had looked different back then. He thought he made the right decision. It had felt right. Now, he doesn't know what to think.

The thoughts and feelings start rushing through him. Too fast, too many. He has to stop his mind from succumbing to these dangerous vibrations or he won't be able to function throughout the night, let alone write his misbegotten paper.

He looks at the clock on his laptop. The basketball game should have started by now. The world is still spinning, time continuously moving. He is still sitting. Funny, he thinks, how that works.

No longer stuck on a topic he begins to write out his paper. He writes about expectations. He writes about loss. He writes about the never-ending gravity of time.

When the sun has set, he finishes. The laptop is closed, the wires are coiled, wrapped, and put away, and he removes himself from the table. The Moe's bag remains behind.

He walks to class, the lights along the walkway coming to life. The night air is cool on his exposed skin, reminding him that Florida will no longer be living up to its name as the Sunshine

State. As he nears the basketball area, he sees people streaming out, cheering with joy. He angles his trajectory to the parking lot, now flooding with people celebrating. Apparently, their team won.

He spots the people clustered around the entrance. Their excitement is evident as they revel in the atmosphere, instruments packed away and carelessly shoved to the side. As he approaches the group, the girl sees him and informs him of the team's victory. "Now the team will be going to playoffs, and we'll get to go with them." Already the rest of the group is making plans for the future and their trip.

He congratulates them on their success, even offers to take pictures to include them all. "It's a big moment," he says, "better not to leave anyone out." The camera snaps, capturing their moment.

DARKNESS

David

Look out the window
What do you see?
Nothing but a vast sea –
Darkness

Look into my eyes
Wide and pleading
Empty as a vast sea -
Darkness

Welcome to my world
The future is dead to me
No hope to see
Empty as a vast sea -
Darkness

Why must it be?
Nothing but darkness inside of me
What went wrong?
All my hope is gone
When all I see is
Empty as a vast sea –
Darkness

BEYOND BARRIERS

Ben

The sun pokes through the trees around 6:45am. A beautiful sunrise turns the sky a glorious reddish-orange color, which should only be observed from a beach-front balcony of a twelfth-floor high-rise condominium, not from the window of a prison dormitory. The loud sound of an officer's voice yelling "count time" creaks at the soul. I cringe at this so frequent occurrence; the pleasurable sensation of sleep interrupted by the demands of a system structured to take inventory of confined men. I feel less than a man being forced to wake and sit up like a puppet on a shelf. I open my eyes to observe the surrounding environment and dread waking up in a 3 by 7 foot bed attached to another bunk. However, the brightness of the day sets the tone of my emotions; I feel whole despite being disconnected from the outside world. I rise and for some strange reason I'm entranced at the window. Few take the time to observe from this position; birds take flight, bring a brief feeling of joy. I long to be at home, living a productive lifestyle, surrounded by family and friends; yet, I'm imprisoned.

I see not only with my eyes but also with my mind. Looking at the system from a positive side allows me to navigate my environment so that I benefit from each day. Avoiding the nonsense and watching things develop beforehand, my mind pushes for productivity. It's discouraging at times to know that the barrier is so close to getting beyond, yet so far at the same time. The distance is stretched by gain time, long sentences, court decisions, appeals, parole board hearings, etc. I listened to an older man repeatedly express that he would not die in prison after having done 41 years, imprisoned since he was 15. His belief in his freedom would manifest into reality when he was considered for early release under the juvenile criminal act. Watching the man leave made me think about all the other men that did not get the chance to walk beyond the barrier, dying in prison. They would be placed in a local grave if their family or friend did not claim their remains. I realize just how blessed I am to have a release date.

Located just outside the southwest corner of my restricted environment sits a small trailer park. Unrestricted people dwelling so close to an inauspicious compound perplexes me. I see them driving cars to their destinations; I notice a woman jogging with her music player. Yearning for an exchange in scenery, I feel awful for allowing my former decisions to dictate my current state.

Trapped where time is the only thing valuable enough to purchase freedom, the passing of time flows with impeccable speed. While lifers walk amongst a stream of yearly releasers, some are content with their situations. Many others cannot bear the separation for long periods of time; suicide becomes an option rather than being confined. Life on the inside is a constant battle for survival, mentally and physically, between officers and inmates. Lives are lost over the simplest things, an argument here, stupidity there, the value of life means little to some.

The punishment is also reflected in the food I'm forced to consume. I'm punished from the 'institutional use only' food products, limited resources, few outdoor activities, overpriced canteen items, no air conditioning, constant degrading, constant humiliation, and so much more. I've never been able to get comfortable in this environment. I refuse to allow the system to institutionalize my existence.

Not physically present in the lives of family and friends, the barrier has hindered communications; thus, incarcerated men are "out of sight out of mind." Connections and communications are severed due to a variety of key factors, one being the duration of one's sentence. The mind must be able to endure the many experiences and the spirit must be at peace within in order to make it out alive and sane. I'm blessed to be in a state of perpetual awareness. My mind wonders, my mind ponders, my eyes observe. I process information from different perspectives. It's confusing to some when I express how I assess the world we share.

This very moment my focus lies on the other side of intertwined grayish metal, topped off with barbed wire. Sadness and hopelessness is all I feel at this moment realizing I am separated from the outside world by mere pieces of metal constructed to ensure I remain bound, forming an emphatic separation of two worlds. One world in constant motion, while my world, in comparison, seems static and repetitious. One side of the barrier considered the inside; the other, the outside, epitomized as freedom. The distance my vision travels is interrupted by the close proximity of pine trees that surround Tomoka Correctional Institution; it gives me the impression of hopelessness and unworthiness, being hidden from public view. In the middle of the woods, I feel like I'm on a distant island in the middle of the Pacific Ocean, isolated. Miles from the nearest town, the prison is strategically located; if one escaped, his or her chances of survival are minimalized and the chances of capture increased.

Like reading a book or watching a movie where your thoughts are captivated by the imagined event, my thoughts are beyond barriers. The smell of grass freshly cut by the inside grounds crew triggers a memory of my old push mower Mother used to make me cut the yard with. I hated it at first, subsequently feeling good finishing what I started. Yet, I'm reminded of my state of incarceration due to the circling of the big white van, occupied by drivers certified to protect the outside from individuals on the inside. All precautions are taken to ensure we remain confined. Corrections officers have the right to shoot and kill anyone who attempts to escape, without regard to the charge or charges an individual may be in prison for. Many have vanished going beyond the barrier.

A grey and black uniform marks the officer's status within this prison system as one who is in authority, while an inmate's uniform, a blue shirt and blue pants, marks him as a criminal. The officers uniform suggests: "I am not you and you will listen to me." Once the officers step into their uniforms, some seem to lose all concern for humanity. They themselves become institutionalized to various degrees. Two officers walk the perimeter checking for signs of escape. Being governed, oppressed, watched, directed, told, forced, worked, fed, clothed, disrespected, emotionally breaks me down at times, leaving it up to me to remain humble through it all.

I stare aimlessly at life outside the realm of imprisonment, knowing my day will come. My children, my siblings, my family, my community are responsibilities that dance around my head. I would love to see my son graduate or my daughter bring home report cards, to attend family holiday gatherings. Life continues on its progressive course, while my life is at a standstill. I know in the future things will be much better for me with society benefiting from my existence. In the distance, through the double 12-foot metal fence lined with motion detectors, I notice a Fed-Ex truck delivering packages to a warehouse. A driver jumps out. I aspire to trade positions with the working man; however, I cannot exchange locations and allow someone to suffer this atrocious condition. Yet viewing this free man doing his job, gives me a sense of relief; it's possible to have a life after incarceration with so many opportunities available. I'm so anxious to get on the other side, having finally gained control over the direction of my life; a poem emerges inside my head:

> As I sit inside these gates behind walls, it is all for a reason,
> As I sit inside these gates behind walls season after season,
> As I sit inside these gates behind walls, freedom awaits
>   teasing, just teasing,
> As I sit inside these gates behind walls, knowing my future,
>   my people, and GOD,
> are what I believe, truly believe in...
> (My Body Is in Prison Not My Mind).

On weekends the vehicles on the outer limits of Tomoka Correctional Institute are mostly occupied by visitors with intentions of stepping inside the realm of imprisonment to show love and support to men who've been deemed unfit to remain in society. Loved ones hug and laugh, smile, kiss, talk, create memorable moments, make positive differences for fenced-in beings. I experience a tremendous amount of relief at visitation. The feeling of being surrounded by family and friends for only a few hours is astounding and stress relieving. Life can seem bad and unfavorable at times, until I get that visit, and joy and happiness enter my soul. But the effects of incarceration reach well beyond the inmate, touching everyone close to him. The amount of time and energy, as well as finances, invested just visiting someone in prison is a hindrance for some. The worst part comes at the end of the visit when the visitor has to return to the outside world only after a few hours, leaving behind a husband, brother, father, son, cousin, or friend. Each weekend I watch the many visitors depart in their cars, leaving with tears, praying this all comes to an end sooner rather than later.

Darkness comes quick when the sun begins its downward descent. The trees once again interrupt the sun's glare. It sets with ease as I watch working families on the other side of the barrier return home from a good day's worth of pay. Pole lights break darkness into segments. This darkness symbolizes the completion of another day; I'm frustrated at spending another twenty-four hours confined.

I look behind me; a disgusting feeling hits me in the core. "I hate this place," I say to myself, trapped like some untamed animal. I notice many inmates trying to deal with their dilemmas as best can be. Men, considered undesirable, packed into dorms constructed to hold sixty to ninety beings for long periods of time, such disgraceful warehousing of people with little to engage themselves in. The overflow of the prison system forced the creation of regulations allowing for these inhuman living conditions. I cannot allow this experience to deteriorate my mind. Quite a few have permitted this environment to hinder their intellectual faculties. They become mental vegetables, leaving them in a state of institutional dependency. Inmates try to deal with their boredom in many ways—reading, writing, watching television. Boredom forces men to deal with each other in some fashion, putting differences aside. I feel out of place. I don't belong here. This is not me. I bury myself in books, attending school, participating in programs and classes, keeping my mind focused on the end goal: gaining the most out of this experience so I never return to this side of the fence once released.

I gaze through the window and I look up at the crescent moon while the stars sparkle in the deep distance. I am connected to God and nature. I'm alone in my own world, not bound by physicalities. I picture myself laying on the ground in the backyard of my home, enjoying the splendid feeling of grass upon my skin, sharing thoughts with my wife and kids about how life has been so good to me, despite all I've been through. Blessed to spend quality time without any limitations.

Once considered a fool, I've transcended. I've broken beyond other barriers; like the labels that have been placed upon me. Thinking of taking a cruise around the world, compels me to remain humble, so I don't extend my time looking from this perspective. My thoughts are interrupted by the flashing of the lights signifying one of the many repetitious count times, demanding I return to my assigned bunk location. The prison system must take stock of its inventory. I glance at the fence once more, and peer beyond the barrier; I'll be free soon.

ATLAS POSE

Roger

> The stark and endless night I haunt,
> For fleeting days I would to know.
> The air, this stillness, heavy, slow.
> A star beckons a wish I own.
> In Atlas pose I stand alone.
>
> The spark of peerless light I taunt,
> For castles in the air do flee.
> Their weight, I know, could shatter me.
> Still I bear on 'til dust from bone.
> In Atlas pose I stand alone.

DR. KING HAD A DREAM BUT I'M LIVING A NIGHTMARE

James

Dr. King had a dream that one day black boys and girls could join hands with white boys and girls on the playgrounds of America, as brothers and sisters, but I'm living a nightmare where kids are being killed at America's schools.

Dr. King had a dream, but I'm living a nightmare.

Dr. King saw an America where a person is not judged by the "color of their skin, but by the content of their character," but I see an America where young people are being killed for wearing the wrong-colored clothing.

Dr. King had a dream, but I'm living a nightmare.

Dr. King saw poverty as a social ill, but I see young women get pregnant just to increase their welfare. Dr. King saw equality, liberty, and justice for all, but I see the penal system full of black males. Where's the "equal justice to balance the scales"?

Dr. King had a dream, but I'm living a nightmare.

Dr. King saw integrated buses, school stores, and restaurants; but I see rival gangs, drug dealers, pushers, and glocks. Dr. King saw united brotherhood, love for all mankind, but I see kids disrespecting their parents, doing drugs, and drinking wine. Dr. King saw strong black families, solid community churches filled of every kind, but I see single mothers, crack houses, and moral decline.

Dr. King had a dream, but I'm living a nightmare.

Dr. King was assassinated in Memphis Tennessee; his leadership, vision, and that dream are a legacy for you and for me. My nightmare will fade with time because the echoes of his screams: "I have a dream, I have a dream, I have a dream."

Dr. King had a dream, now help me end this nightmare.

HOPE (IN A PRISON VISITATION ROOM)

Roger

Love somehow abounds here,
Though stained by uncertain hope,
and longing for the ability to cope
with the day-to-day.

Although dreams now remain,
sands of time slide away.
We hold fast to the reflections of the past—
Shining through eyes amist—
broken vessels a-list on the sea.

What will become of them? What of me?
Will the tides of change separate?
Should I cast my anchor
Or allow them to drift free?

For try as we may,
time always brings change,
and what's lost are not only the dreams, unattained,
but the joy of the moment that's there to gain.

Lost within the revelries of yesterday,
not to be fully appreciated, is the here and now.
Today's delicate hope,
Overshadowed by yesterday's cloud.

red(s)

\ red \ — *noun*

redness (the chromatic color resembling the hue of blood); emotionally charged terms used to refer to extreme radicals or revolutionaries; loss, red ink "the company operated in the red last year"

\ red \ — *adjective*

of a color at the end of the color spectrum (next to orange); crimson, violent; red-faced, flushed, reddened or suffused with or as if with blood from emotion or exertion

ANONYMITY

Marcus

I like the loneliness . . . alone in holiness.

Unknown and holding this . . . scepter in chains.

Hated by humanity cause I'm a diamond in flames,
------
burning through the lies that keep us trapped in these planes.

You're so oblivious to these treacherous games.

They call me Satan, hate'n, say'n that I worship demons.

Look at their racist faces; faith is what backs up their reasons.

Democracy and the masses murdered Jesus.

They voted to elect his death who birthed our thesis.

The Holy One of Israel that brought us out of Egypt.

The Morning Star is what I Am and yet they call me evil.

A broken piece of the body which makes the whole loaf.

I raise my chalice to the Sun and make that cold toast.

No Electrical resistance with the Holy Ghost.

Interactive attraction's what forms electron pairs.

------

temperatures below zero too cold for Polar Bears.

But you gotta go that low to know that code
to enter the heart

------

and it gets real dark

------

real, real dark

------

till you hit that mark and you see that light and you're
lit up real bright and you sit up all night say'n,
"I can't sleep."

Now you're living your dream. Awake in your dream.
No taking your dream. Your thoughts on the screen.
Impossible things can happen if we . . .

Believe

Believe in the fire of love in your mind that shoots up
your spine. I'm more than my crime, I'm more than
my blues, can't walk in my shoes, I know how to lose,
I know what I've lost, I'm pay'n my cost, I'm
ready to win, no play and pretend. I'll tell you
again,

Believe.

THE MARIANNA BREAKDOWN

John K.

for all the boys sent to Arthur G. Dozier school

One wet day in January I see the words crawl across the screen
    slow and nasty like a moccasin in the grass,
    fat as a child's forearm, rotten-fish stink
    to water your eyes maybe to warn:
"55 more found at Florida boys' home notorious for—"
    I look away, a chill easing down my back.

The woods behind the Dozier school soaked up its secrets
    one bloody drop at a time, ad hoc justice dispensed
    by calloused country hands, sunburned and liver-spotted,
    in the shed the survivors called the white house.
Unseen, the awful tide seeped through the scrub oak and palmetto
    To lap at the doorsteps of whitewashed clapboard houses.

It's hard busting a living out of this poor sandy soil.
    What we do for the State of Florida, I don't think on it that much.
        I know it beats chopping cotton all to hell.

Nothing grows right over those oblong patches out back—
    was it your backyard they dug up fifty-something dead boys in,
    it'd be on the TV for a month of Sundays and your face too,
    right alongside those faded old crinkled Kodaks
        some mama's lost hope riding in her billfold
        if they even had mamas at all.
    Nobody's gonna miss those little bastards anyhow.

Mostly those kids was just throwed away
    and we had to catch hold of them

spitting and struggling and clawing
like the last of that litter I put in a croaker sack
Saturday morning before my daughters got up.
Ain't that different, what happens sometimes.

Excepting those forgotten mamas and long-dead granny women,
        who even remembers them boys?
    Sure ain't no picture postcards at the Welcome Center
    bragging on this crop to sour your free cup of OJ from
            the Sunshine State.
                        They had to be showed who was the boss.
                        The Good Book says spare the rod spoil the child.
                        We stand by that.
                        No monsters here nor haunted houses—
                        you want that, go see Disney.
                        I'm done talking about it.
                        No-one saw a thing.

What the hell did you expect from bad seed?

IF I CAN LEND YOU MY MIND

James

I'm sick of babies dying, and mothers crying, daddy locked up in prison, lying.

What kind of world are we living in?

Bishops molesting children but aren't sent to the pen. AK 47's rule our blocks. In the Supreme Court the NRA wins. Afghanistan a mess, the pres. had to change generals; more guns in my hood simply means more funerals.

If I can lend you my mind.

You will feel my pain. A born-again believer, a self-taught king. An over-achiever. A father who misses his kids, though they are grown. A prison sentence that was deserved, but way too long. A family man with roots, momma hang on—I'll be there when you need me. A Christian society with vengeful hearts—I'm redeemed but they don't believe me.

If I can lend you my mind.

Minorities having to fight for rights, malnutrition killing babies, prisoners thrown away forever, I find this so amazing. We find money for wars, we build electric cars, at 12 and 13 we put our children behind bars. And then we wonder why they kill each other. In prison they enter as young boys, but others try to make them mothers, you don't ask, you don't tell; I won't take that any further.

If I can lend you my mind.

G-code all lies, brothers telling on each other, so stop this gangsta shit before it goes any further. Speaking the truth, I gave you my mind. There's millions of brothers just like me, they just gave up trying. Someone stand up so we can find a way to be free, instead of holding up this mantle called 'menace to society.'

If I can lend you my mind.

How we going to stay out the pen when we can't diagnose the problem? Education is the key. You should be studying for hours. Join CEP at Stetson and pray God changes your ways. Be thankful for the simple things and give God all your praise. Each one teach one is all I demand. Most brothers will listen, they have no other plans.

If I can lend you my mind.

Check me out, I was just like you, a brother who acted a fool. I thought robbing and taking shit was exciting and cool. After 30 years in this place with people telling me what to do, I'm sharing my mind with you, so you don't have to go through what I went through. I would do anything to walk up to my momma's door, kiss her on the cheek as I watch her tears flow, sit down at her table and eat a decent meal. Do you have any idea how that would make me feel?

If I can Lend you mind.

King would say don't give up; the dream lives on. Malcolm would say by any means necessary, learn all you can. Tubman would say get ready; I'm coming for you, son. Momma would say I'm praying baby; keep your head up.

If I can lend you my mind.

BURNT SUGAR

Ken

1835 The Florida Territory

The sun was still low in the sky, barely peeking through the tops of the pine trees that surrounded the plantation. The lawn glimmered with the fresh dew of the morning giving the impression that each individual blade of grass was weeping for what it was about to witness. Qua was bound to an old oak tree by a thin, worn-out piece of leather; it seemed he was hugging a long-lost family member. His arms were stretched taut and the lean muscles of his back stood prominent against his skin.

The overseer of the plantation, Mr. Shelton, stood about twelve feet away uncoiling a whip and was glaring from under a mop of red curls that were mashed down by his hat. His severe countenance silenced any discussion about the bloody task being carried out.

Qua was naked except for a woolen loincloth. Beads of nervous sweat had formed on every inch of his six-foot frame. Although he had been fortunate enough not to have experienced the whip firsthand, he knew what to expect. He had witnessed plenty, including his wife's three months prior. Mr. Shelton had assigned him fifteen lashes for getting caught talking to the Seminoles the night before after being forbidden to do so.

The words, "I'll learn you to mind me, boy," were the only warning he received before the first lash fell. It unleashed such an ear-splitting "crack," a covey of quail hiding in deep grass about a hundred yards away took flight. No matter what he had seen or thought, nothing could have prepared him for the impact of that first lash as his skin split apart and a welt equal to the size of the leather thong rose up. Time stopped and all the air in his lungs emptied on the back of a scream that was so inhuman, the other slaves who were forced to watch gave a collective gasp. The remaining fourteen lashes rained down on him ceaselessly. The overseer completed his task methodically and devoid of any emotion, as if he was performing the most menial of tasks. For Qua, the 2 to 3 minutes that it took to finish this torture seemed like an hour. His back felt as if someone had dumped hot coals all over it. His throat was raw from screaming and his legs were shaking so uncontrollably that if he had not been tied to the tree, he would have crumpled to the ground. The dirt and grass surrounding the tree were sprinkled with a mixture of his blood and sweat in a pattern of macabre artistry.

"Rosie, cut him down and clean 'im up," Mr. Shelton yelled at Qua's sister who was standing in horror. "I want 'im back to work in the morning. The rest of you stop gawking and act like there is work to be done or you'll be next." Rosie and her husband, Scipio, immediately rushed over to Qua and cut him loose from his bonds as Mr. Shelton stalked off toward the mill.

Once back in their hut, Rosie attended to his wounds and spoke to him in a quiet, admonishing manner. "I told you to leave them Indians be, no good can come from you all's plans."

Despite the stinging pain caused by Rosie washing his wounds, Qua responded with the same stubborn attitude that ended with him tied to a tree. "I know what I's doin'. I believe in John and Wild Cat, they's goin to see all of us free and make that bastard Shelton pay. Just wait and you see, sis."

"I just hope you all's plans don't see you dead first," she replied while continuing to dab at his wounds.

With great effort Qua slowly lifted himself up and turned to look at his sister with determined eyes, "We's already dead 'cause this ain't livin; doin' what we doin' every day, for what? I don't even have Milly anymore."

As he whispered these last words his eyes changed from resolve to melancholy. Qua had not spoken of Milly, his wife, to Rosie since she was whipped and sold to the Rees plantation by Mr. Shelton for physically rebuffing his sexual advances. Rosie could not imagine being separated from Scipio, so she never spoke to him about his loss. She regretted that, as the weight and pain of their separation was so very clear in his eyes.

"We'll get through this. The Lord knows we've had harder times. Milly will be fine; I hear that Massa Forrester is a gentle boss and nothin' like Massa Shelton. You got to have faith." She said these words to Qua's back. He had already laid down again. He did not want her to see the tears that were so freely running down his face.

Life without his wife did not seem worth living. Every day the pain of their separation rose up anew as he imagined hearing her laugh floating somewhere on the breeze or he would catch the faintest hint of her aroma in their shack. Too many times he had turned around expecting her to be right there smiling at him in that special way she reserved just for him. Now, because of John Caesar, he had a real hope of reuniting with Milly. No matter how small that chance was, he was going to take it and any risk associated with it. He felt they had made the mistake of "having faith" and not acting when they had a chance to escape on their march from the Ormond Plantation twelve years ago. Instead, they heeded his mother's advice about trusting and waiting on the

Lord to do his work. Look where that had gotten them: Mama dead from yellow fever, Milly sold off to another plantation, and he and his sister working in the fields mercilessly from sun-up to sundown on a sugar plantation. No! As bad as he missed Mama and wanted to fulfill her wishes, he was going to fight for his family now. Rosie had finished cleaning his wounds and left him in the hut alone thinking about how he ended up here.

* * *

The only thing he knew for sure about his birth was that he was born on a Thursday. He knew that because that is what Qua meant in the West African dialect of his parents. By following his mama's word, he now counted nineteen summers. He and his sister were born into slavery, unlike their parents who were native to Guinea. They were kidnapped from their village by raiding parties and sold to Captain Cook of the Christiana, a slaver that plied the transatlantic slave routes. Somehow, they managed to survive the horrors of the Middle Passage on that slaver and found port at Fernandina in Spanish-owned Florida. They were bought as part of a group and put to work on Captain Ormond's Plantation, with his father processing sugar cane and his mother doing kitchen duties. Within a year they were given permission to be married and the births of Rosie and Qua soon followed. They felt that God had finally begun to hear their broken cries.

Then reality for a slave family struck like lightning. When Qua was just seven years old, Ben, a field hand, fought with and killed the Captain while trying to run away. Such an unspeakable act caused a furious and deadly reaction from the surrounding community. The memory from that night would forever be etched into Qua's mind. The whites indiscriminately tore through the slave houses, taking liberty with the women and beating whomever they felt deserved it. Accused of conspiring, his father and four other slaves were hung. The bodies were left hanging from the tree as a warning to anyone else thinking about trying the same thing. His family was not even allowed to bury his father. They were sold to the Cruger-Depeyster plantation as the Ormond family quickly liquidated their estate and fled back to their homeland of Scotland.

Since then, he had been doing the back-breaking work of cutting and crushing cane on this 600-acre plantation under the strict, abusive rule of John Shelton. It was one of the smallest sugar plantations in the East Florida district and was composed of an L-shaped sugar works building that contained a boiling house and purgery with a separate building to the side for the steam engine. The overseer's house was a clapboard style that had one main room with two connecting living quarters on each side. It was about fifty feet long and had large windows in front and back that allowed the Florida heat to escape easily. The front porch appeared to have been made in a rush by an inexperienced carpenter as boards were not joined properly and the step was off kilter. The twelve single-room slave huts, which housed all of the plantation's seventy-eight slaves, were laid out in a semicircle pattern around the main cooking house.

Mr. Shelton took over as manager because the owners of the plantation, whom Qua had never seen, were from New York and knew nothing about plantation life. He hated them because they chose to stay up north, reaping the benefits of the black person's labor while avoiding directly participating in their inhumane treatment. He felt that if you were going to take everything from a man, then you should at least have the guts to look him in the eye and let him know that you are doing it. He had dreamt every night about running away with Milly and raising a family as free people. All this seemed to be a dream, until one lonely night, the decision to walk because the pain of losing Milly forbid him from sleeping, changed his future forever.

"Qua!" When he heard his name whispered from the dark, he froze and listened intently to the woods around him. All he could hear was the pounding of his heart and the buzzing of mosquitos in his ears. He searched with his eyes, but the moonlit foliage revealed nothing.

"Qua!" There it was again! Hearing his name this time did not soothe his curiosity but created a flurry of butterflies in his stomach instead. Why was someone whispering his name from the trees? Who were they and what did they want? He began to plot out a path to run if things started to go bad.

Suddenly, he felt a light touch on his shoulder and at the same time heard the words, "I'm right here."

All the plans of an escape proved worthless. Every muscle in his body froze and his feet became as immobile as if they had sprouted roots. It took all his concentration just to get the air in his lungs to squeeze past his heart which was lodged in his throat. With his eyes leading the way, he slowly turned his head toward the voice, to see a black man dressed like an Indian standing just two feet away! He was laughing so softly that at first Qua thought he was growling.

Adrenaline raced through Qua's body as the man moved from beside him to in front and said, "No need to worry, Qua. I'm your friend."

Although these words began to unravel some of the knots that his muscles had become, they did little to answer any one of the hundred questions that came to his mind. Who are you? How do you know my name? And most importantly, how on God's green earth did you get so close without me hearing you? Before he could ask any one of these, the man sat down on an old log about ten feet away. He looked at Qua with a huge smile that was highlighted by large, brown eyes that were kind and gentle. This had a disarming effect on Qua. He relaxed and started assessing the man before him. His hair was beginning to gray and he had crow's feet around his eyes when he smiled. He was taller than Qua and skinnier too, but not in a way that indicated poor nourishment. He held himself with an assuredness that spoke of an inner strength. His sitting pose reminded Qua of a cat who was preparing to pounce, but it was the eloquence in which he spoke that proved that he was not some common man.

"I am aware that you do not know who I am, but you do know my wife, Patience. She keeps me informed about everything and everybody at your plantation. I know what happened to you and your family and would like to offer a proposal for your consideration."

Qua just stood still with a bewildered look on his face until he realized the man was waiting for a response. "Who is you?"

The man continued to look at Qua with that contagious smile for a few moments, then replied, "I apologize for not introducing myself properly. I am John Caesar and I represent the Seminole tribe. Maybe you have seen some of us moving around from time to time since we hunt these lands."

"I seen Indians 'fore, but you's black," Qua stammered in response.

John broke out into such a fit of honest laughter that Qua joined in his merriment and did not even know why. When John had recovered from his outbreak, he leveled his eyes that were full of compassion at Qua and said, "Sometimes I forget how out of touch plantation slaves can be. Well, let me tell you, there are many black Seminoles and even more black people that live with the Seminoles or under the protection of the micco or chief. Some are runaways that pay a tribute and some are free, but all are welcome. Another thing you probably don't know, there are all-black villages where not one person living in them has ever experienced slavery, only freedom. They have lived their lives in peace and prosperity completely outside the control of the whites."

Qua was dumbstruck, black Seminoles? Free blacks? How was this possible?

John continued, "Unfortunately, they say a treaty has now been made between the tribe and the white man's President. In it we supposedly gave away our land here and agreed to move out west among the Creek nation. The problem is, Micanopy, the chief of all the Seminoles says he didn't sign anything. Advising him is Yasi Aholo, an influential warrior, who is pushing for open war. He has a large part of the nation behind him and they are vowing to resist. This group includes my chief, Emathla."

Qua continued to gape. Treaties? What does any of that have to do with him?

As if reading his mind, John began to explain, "The black people among the tribe were the first to join up with resistance. Fighting is the only option that allows us to control our own destiny. You see, whites from all over are trespassing on our lands. They lie, kidnap, and murder in order to put us in slavery. Out west, Jim Boy and Paddy Carr, two influential chiefs among the Creeks are making noise and promising to make trouble when we get there. For some reason they feel that we are their rightful property. Only the Seminoles are respecting who we are as a people. They are willing to fight for us, but we are few and the whites are many. This is why I am here tonight, talking to you. I need your help."

"How can I help you? I's a slave."

While shaking his head, John again began to laugh in his slow and quiet manner before answering, "You are more powerful than you realize. Think about this, at any moment there are over seventy blacks living on your plantation. How many whites? What, maybe six or seven? What do you think would happen if you helped me to convince all those people to throw down their tools and fight back?"

Qua's stomach knotted up and his hands became clammy as flashes of white men with guns and his father hanging from a tree came flooding back. Qua's response was hurried and his voice shrill, "We can't. They have guns. They'll kill all of us. You don't know how mean Massa Shelton is, he'd kill you too."

John fixed Qua with such a lethal gaze that it sent a chill down his spine. "Stronger and more resourceful men than your Massa Shelton have tried to kill me without much luck."

Although Qua had dreamt every night about freedom and thought about killing Mr. Shelton many times over, he never imagined that one act could lead to the success of the other. How could that be possible? How many times had he seen other slaves run only to get caught and have their punishment put on full display in front of everyone? Too many nights he laid awake hearing their screams. Whatever horrid manner of chastisement the master dreamt up, it was always prolonged and bloody. He knew white people were not human; only monsters could commit acts like that on another human being. How does a person escape monsters? No, white people were the ones in power. It's just how things were.

As if reading his mind John said, "The power that the whites have is not as secure as you think. We are uniting in resistance against them. Yasi Ahola has declared there is a blood debt to be paid. We want you to join us. We want all the slaves to join us. Tell me, how many times a day do you think of Milly? If you help us, I promise, not only will you get Milly back, but you can pay back your Massa for all he has done to you. So, will you help me unite the slaves on your plantation and take back from the white man what is rightfully ours?"

For Qua, this question was like being dowsed with a bucket of cold spring water on a hot summer's day. There was not anything in life that he wanted more than to live free with Milly and now a chance was here and all he could do was gape like some fool at the man offering help. It was panic that finally broke him out of his stupor. Fear of John walking away, leaving him here to a life of slavery without his wife, surged through his body. These emotions swept aside any concern of punishment or death like a leaf in a hurricane. He met John's eyes and uttered one word. "Yes."

John directed Qua to contact Patience so he could be brought up to date on everything already happening at the plantation. Qua had known Patience since they arrived here, and she had always been kind to him and Rosie. She was short and wiry with the dark skin and curved back of someone that had spent years on the rows picking cotton. He was surprised to learn that she was involved in this plan. She always seemed so timid and obedient. Qua quickly learned that people are not always who they seem to be.

* * *

He did not know what hurt worse, the kick to the chest that landed him flat on his back gasping for breath or the fact that a small woman did it. Patience was standing over him staring with the same lethal gaze he saw on John the night before. He had made the mistake of laughing when Patience suggested she take the lead instead of him. He had barely finished the words, "But you's just a girl," before he found himself looking at the ceiling of the hut.

"You know nothin', boy. Me and John seen and done things that'd make you piss your britches."

Adding insult to injury, Ben and Tom, two fellow slaves that were sitting on the floor watching all this, were laughing non-stop. Ben was a giant of a man; his perfectly round head was bald, and his large cheeks made his eyes appear small and slightly sunken. Mr. Shelton used him exclusively in the crushing room where all the work was heavy and taxing. Tom was quite the opposite; he was short and rotund with a full head of hair that sprung up in every direction. He had one cocked eye that was the source of never-ending amusement for the other slaves. Although they were polar opposites in appearance, they were identical in their jovial demeanor and nigh to inseparable as friends. Other than the fact that they found his humiliation funny, he was glad they were here. Patience had taken a few steps back to allow Qua room to stand up. As the burn of shame receded from his cheeks and his breathing returned to normal, he reflected on Patience's words. She was wrong. He did know something, and he was worth the confidence John had placed in him. If they did not want him, fine, so be it, but he was going to tell them how he felt first.

"I may be young and not seen as much as you, but that doesn't mean I's not tired of how things are. My work fills their table while I quietly go to bed at night with hunger as my friend. I's stood by as my mama got beat bloody cuz the mistress was jealous of the master's looks. My daddy was strung up for someone else's wrong. My sister was held down so the white man could take his pleasure. My blood and sweat rains down on those fields out there while others gets the money."

As these words fell from his mouth, the shame he felt a few moments earlier was replaced with something brand new for Qua—purpose.

"I's tired of just standin' by while that son of a bitch has his way. He stole my wife from me, and all I did was let the straw soak up my tears at night. My days of lookin' away as I's treated like less than a man, no, less than human are over. If you's don't want me to fight with you, then fine; I'll find my own way. But one thing's for sure, I's fighting. I ain't no coward, and I's gonna get Milly back and we's gonna be free."

Ben and Tom had ceased laughing, and Patience stood with her hands on her hips and a bright smile on her face. "Well, well. It looks like good ol' John was right again. I wasn't sure 'bout you, till now."

Tears had begun to roll down Qua's face, and his hands were shaking. Giving voice to all those events in his life for the first time had unleashed a flood of emotions that he could not control. All three of them slowly gathered around Qua to place a reassuring hand on him or give a nod of the head as a sign of understanding. For the first time since Milly was taken away, he felt that he had a reason to live. They did not discuss any plans that night but shared stories together that cemented their newly-formed bond.

In the beginning, they were cautious about which other slaves were brought into their circle out of fear that someone would tell Mr. Shelton about their plans. He had already warned all the slaves that if they were caught talking to any Indians, they would be whipped. As if taking that threat as an invitation, John and other warriors, including Emathla, began showing up to their secret gatherings to make sure things were progressing. When Qua spoke at these meetings, the same fire of belief that burned in his eyes that first night with Patience shone just as bright, affecting everyone including some Seminole warriors. One in particular, Coacoochee or Wild Cat, Emathla's son, was caught up by one such speech and felt compelled to share with the slaves why the Seminoles were fighting.

His regal presence commanded the attention of the group as he stood up. Three eagle feathers hung from his head scarf, and a silver crucifix dangled from his neck. His red leggings and sleeveless vest were contrasted by a white sash wrapped around his waist. What impressed everyone most, though, was the large scalping knife that rested at his side.

He began slow and deliberate in his speech, "For more than a hundred summers has the Seminole warrior rested in the cool shade of the oak. The sun of a hundred winters has risen upon his ardent chase of the bear and deer, and no one has questioned his right or disputed his range. The white man lives in towns, where a thousand people run about in a great hurry over a small piece of land. The Seminole swims rivers, runs and jumps over logs with his rifle in hand in pursuit of food. The great Spirit is the author of this difference and each people is in his own place. The white man does not respect this order and always looks to possess what others have. He wants to have his way with us as he has the black man. He desires to steal our land and our heritage as he has yours and send us west to an unknown place among unfriendly tribes who seek to do us harm. We will not allow him to make us black but will make him red with blood and then blacken him in the sun and rain, where the wolf shall smell of his bones, and the buzzard live upon his flesh."[1]

---

[1] Parts of this speech were taken from a talk delivered to E. Wanton and Horatio S. Dexter, on the 24th of May, 1821 by Micanopy, head chief of the Seminole Indians.

The last part was said with such vehemence the group was left speechless. The burning in Qua's chest for vengeance had become a righteous flame. He looked around and saw the same light in everyone else's eyes. Afterwards, he sought out Wild Cat and asked him many questions concerning the Seminoles. Through this conversation and many more after, he learned about the depredations the whites committed upon their tribe.

Soon, a friendship was formed, and Qua risked punishment every night so they could talk. Growing up Qua did not have many friends, so the bond that developed with Wild Cat was special. That feeling was shown to be mutual as Wild Cat promised to help him and John recover Milly and invited them to live with him and his people in the village of Tohopekilika. They sealed their pact in blood and swore to fight at each other's side against the whites as brothers. The other slaves saw this relationship and began looking upon Qua as their de facto leader. They gravitated towards him and wanted to be near when he spoke.

Soon they had enlisted enough help that they felt their plans would be successful. John and just three other warriors came early one morning to finalize arrangements for an advance party of warriors to be hidden. They set Christmas Eve as the day for action because the slaves were given the day off from work, plus any assembly would not draw unwanted attention. Unfortunately for Qua, when one of the warriors, Cho Hadjo, heard that everything was ready, he got excited and let out a whoop that was heard across the plantation. Mr. Shelton, who normally was not walking the slave huts at this time happened to be doing just that and saw Qua and the four Seminoles. The Seminoles hastily made their escape leaving Qua alone to answer for the transgression.

Even though Mr. Shelton and his whip got the best of him today and had him lying in bed with a sore back, he was still sure of one thing. The fire still burned, and he was determined, now more than ever, to show that bastard exactly what he was made of. He would be ready.

* * *

He was not ready!

Today was Christmas Eve and there was still so much to do. Too many people were looking at him for guidance that he suddenly felt unqualified to give, and now he had been delivered the worst possible news. That nosy, tattle-tale Nancy, Mrs. Shelton's house maid, had caused an uproar by telling how she saw Indians with painted faces talking to some slaves during the Christmas dance held on the Hunter plantation last night. Of course, any white person knew that a painted warrior meant violence was not far away. As a precaution, the white women and children along with the house slaves were being evacuated to Colonel Dummett's larger plantation across the river. With all that extra movement, the advance party of Seminole warriors that had been hiding in the slave huts since last night were getting restless. They began pacing back and forth with murder in their eyes, which made everyone around them extremely nervous. How could something so well-planned get so messed up? Just as this thought crossed Qua's mind he heard a familiar voice yelling toward the overseer's house.

"Hello! Is anyone here and about? I am looking to trade some cattle and horses that I have up the road." Seated atop a palomino mare, John was facing the house, dressed only in a pair of tan deerskin leggings and knee-high moccasin boots. The feather hanging from his headband laid across his back which was covered with scars, proving he was no stranger to battle or the whip. He was trying to lure Mr. Shelton out with the promise of a deal so they could ambush him, but to Qua's dismay he was now on guard for anything unusual and refused to come out. Qua stood about a hundred yards off, transfixed on the scene playing out in front of him, silently willing Mr. Shelton to open that door. His heart was so consumed with hate for slavery that it radiated from him in waves. The anticipation of Mr. Shelton's death, which would signal an end of that reality for him, had his attention, so he did not notice the warriors slowly removing themselves from the huts and taking up positions that afforded them clear lines of fire on the house.

Suddenly, a warrior pierced the air with an undulating war scream that made Qua's blood run cold. It was immediately followed by a thunderous volley of musket shot that left him disoriented. John had jumped off his horse and was running for cover as a hail of balls fell upon the house, opening holes in the wooden planks and smashing through windows. The second round of fire was equally deafening and destructive as more Seminoles began to appear and contribute to the barrage. Qua was shaking off the shock of the initial attack when he felt a chorus of screams as the slaves poured out or their shacks. Some were armed with large knives used for cutting cane while others had picked up anything that could be used as a weapon. They quickly surged past the Seminole line and tore into every building on the plantation.

Qua joined the group that consumed the house, focused on one goal, finding Mr. Shelton. He looked down and saw that he had pulled out his fish knife but could not remember when. Anticipation continued to clutch at him as he rushed in. He noticed the back door was wide open, and his heart began to sink. The realization that Mr. Shelton had escaped started to set in as he quickly searched the house. The other slaves were busy ransacking the belongings that were left behind as he stood at the back door staring out in disbelief. Looking out at the plantation and at the other buildings, he saw how the others were starting to meander and knew in his heart that they were too late. Everyone was gone! How could this be? His promised revenge had been stolen from him! Despondency threatened to engulf him as he thought about the injustice of his life.

Patience's voice suddenly sliced into his thoughts, "Hey, Qua!" He looked up and saw her standing outside of a group that had encircled a tree. She was motioning for him to come to her. He hurried over, and as he drew near he could hear the unmistakable sound of flesh being pummeled by fists.

"Where you been, boy?" she asked. "You're missing all the fun."

His heart leapt at the thought that maybe Mr. Shelton had been caught after all. He anxiously pushed his way through the gathered crowd praying it was him. In the middle of the makeshift ring he saw two field hands, Bob and Cuffy, taking turns slugging a white man that was tied to a tree.

While one punched, the other taunted, "Come on, pick up the pace! You're so lazy; how we gonna get any work done?!"

At first Qua did not recognize who it was because his face had been disfigured so badly from the beating. It struck him when he heard their taunts that it was Mr. Gould, the mechanic for the steam engine that ran the cane press. He continued to watch, hoping to achieve some sense of satisfaction from this man's torture. Slowly his stomach started to turn instead. Visions of slaves being tortured by the whites popped into his head, and he wondered to himself, what is the difference in that and what we are doing? Were they any better? As if answering that question, three Seminoles, with Wild Cat leading, broke through the circle and interrupted the display.

Wild Cat looked at the crowd and spoke in a commanding tone, "We are not like the white man; we are warriors. We do not act in this manner. We kill or take prisoner; we do not beat for pleasure."

He then turned and in one swift movement lifted Mr. Gould's head by the hair and ran his knife across his throat, opening a gaping wound that drained his life in seconds. He walked out of the circle in the same manner that he entered. Everyone was stunned into silence. Qua felt the world tilt. He then turned to the side and vomited on the lawn.

Patience was soon at his side patting his back and quietly speaking into his ear, "You'll soon learn, boy. Freedom has a price."

With the plantation removed of all the white people and now securely in the hands of the slaves, a celebration began. Anything of value that remained was taken and dispersed amongst the revelers. The Seminoles had begun to share in the merriment by creating a bonfire and dancing in their ritual manner after a victory. Mr. Shelton's stash of whiskey was discovered, and the festivities moved into full swing.

Qua sat under an old oak tree and refused to join. He was sulking over the fact that Mr. Shelton had escaped. John walked up and sat down close by on a giant root that had grown out of the soil.

Qua did not give any hint of recognition to the intrusion until John asked, "Why are you over here by yourself and not celebrating like everyone else?"

Qua slowly lifted his head and John saw that his face wore a mask of pain. Tears threatened to escape his eyes. In a voice that contained all the despair he felt, he responded, "You promised me revenge. You promised me freedom. How can I ever hope for either now that bastard is still alive and out of my reach?"

John's face had a puzzled look as he tried to make sense of the question, "I apologize if I don't fully understand your question. Yes, Shelton got away today, an unfortunate occurrence indeed. But what does that have to do with your freedom?"

Qua jumped up and stared at John with an incredulous look, "How can you not see?! He owns me. Long as he lives, I's his!"

John shook his head and laughed quietly while Qua continued to stare waiting for an answer. When he first met John, he found that smile and laugh endearing and slightly contagious, but right now it was absolutely irritating. John gave a sigh and a nod of the head as if speaking to himself in his head, "It's easy to forget how young you are and how new the world must seem to you. May I ask you something? What do you perceive freedom to be?"

This question was the last thing Qua was expecting and caused him to shrink back a little from the resolute stance he had assumed. After a few minutes of wrestling with this he replied, "I dunno. I guess havin' my wife and bein' able to come and go as I please. Maybe ownin' a piece a land, somethin' I could call mine. Workin' it with my hands and earnin' my way."

John again nodded to himself, "Those are fine things for sure and are certainly what most men seek. In my life, I have found that word means different things for different people. The Seminoles would never understand this concept of owning land. The whites only feel free when not only owning land, but people as well. My mother was a slave and didn't even own the shirt on her back, but she was the freest person I have ever known. Do you know why?"

Qua, who had sat back down, shook his head in response. "Because she was free on the inside. You see, it didn't matter to her what some white man with a piece of paper said. She knew nobody could ever own who she was as a person. They couldn't tell her what type of mother to be or how to choose between doing right or wrong. She always remained master of the most important choices. No one can ever take that from you either, Qua. You have inspired and led dozens of people on a successful rebellion. Milly sees you as her husband, Wild Cat and Rosie as their brother, and I consider you my friend. We have a greater claim to you than Shelton ever did. If you ask me, you are freer than him. You have made the choice to throw off your chains and take control of your life. Not many people, free or not, can say that."

The tears that had threatened to escape Qua's eyes earlier now moistened his face. "I's such a fool."

John moved to Qua's side and allowed him to work through his emotions before saying, "Trust me, I have made my share of mistakes, with a lot worse consequences than a few tears, too. What matters is who you choose to be from this moment forward. You are free Qua. Now, who are you going to be?"

Author's Note: This is an excerpt from a larger work. Although this story is a work of fiction, it is based upon real people and events that occurred in East Florida in 1835. While researching the causes of the Second Seminole War, I discovered that Black Seminoles and recently liberated enslaved people played an integral role in the war and how it was executed by the United States military. I created Qua and his story with the hope that the reader could catch just a glimpse into the humanity of a people struggling to achieve what is guaranteed by the constitution: freedom.

LAST SIP, MUDDY WELL

John K.

Father, I stand in fear of failing you again.
I could not stop your cries as you walked sleepless
        through the ringing silence of the family-less home.
That horrible year was my end's beginning
        my first trip into another's hell,
        loyal to the one I looked up to.
I chose to stay there, yet no matter my need, you were lost to me
        as you drank, drew away, receding from view and sanity
        right before my eyes.
I kept watch for the instructions:
        what to do with shot-out glass, smashed furniture—
my comforting lie of a safe harbor
gone like the wife and kids.
A finer life than those of my mildly pitiable peers
(I couldn't explain you to them either.)

My road wasn't paved with good intentions.
The cliff-face crumbled as the rules gave way.
Falling boulders, landslides, no exit in sight—
        couldn't you have spared a bit of your grown-up's power,
        that vaunted adult supervision, to show me a way out?
Nope. Your model didn't come with a compass.

Besides, your wallet-waving magic
        brought us to our feet cheering, time and again.
        (Thanks for the economics lesson: reckless abandon
        is more fun than saving, any day of the week.)
Why have credit or credibility if you're not going to use it up?

Don't stop at zero—there's plenty of fuel for this bonfire of the
    vanities.
Flung into the flames: boats, cars, groves, friendships—
    A Viking funeral joylessly consuming the brave captain
    with all that remained of his small-town glory.
I went on that ride straight to the bottom,
    Half-baked and hapless (but loyal—don't forget that part.)

I had boots, now: never felt stronger than when I was striding
    across some long empty concrete space
    heels striking confident echoing notes
    the thrill to come certain to be better
    than the last clench-gripped experience
    standing taller than my timid friends
    gentle souls that they were.
How arrogant: The Fool redux, carefree under Fortune's smiling
sun.

My romance with darkness drove them away as surely
    as your odious self-serving sorrows
    made strangers of everyone we'd known.
    (Another useful lesson: real friends will endure endless drama—
    test them regularly in case they're wavering.)
Good thing you could find so many new folks relaxing in bars
    just waiting for boon companions to discover them.

A sapling needs ample space, else it won't grow upright.
This acorn didn't fall far enough from the tree.
It lay fallow far longer than is normal,
    but the Maker of both acorn and oak
    is not bound by normalcy, blessed be,
    and if the rotted trunk blocked the light for a season or ten,
    it is light's function to enter darkness.

LOVE, LAUGHTER, AND PAIN

Marcus

JOURNAL ENTRY - VOL. 7 #1 SELFLESSNESS
TUESDAY, NOVEMBER 26, 2019

I was in the dish pit talking to "Joey" about doing time. He was biting at the air like a dog that missed the Frisbee, explaining how long he'd experienced freedom in the last twenty-two years. The total was one year. Two six-month bites in twenty-two years, and he's fifty. Doesn't look it or act like it, not the stereotypical fifty-year-old. White guy, tats all over his face and head. It's art. Extreme to most, but it really is art. The most eye catching to me is the backwards handicap symbol under his right eye.

Joey: I like my women like I like my cars.

Being that prison in Florida treats us like we are in middle school, I can't finish our conversation for this entry. Lots of cocaine and sex. Which can easily explain the six-month glimpses of freedom. This last case landed him fifteen mandatory for strong-armed robbery. He was going around hitting people with a baseball bat.

Joey: Not in the head. Not in the head. It was the back. I did two of 'em while she drove and she told on me. I'm not mad at her.

He was hanging out of the window of the passenger side of the car knocking people down to take their valuables. Why? He needed drugs, and his habit cost more than what he made.

Why can't the legislators realize that drugs are the source of 90% of crime? And they want to give non-violent drug offenders relief?[1] We all deserve relief if that's the case, because drugs cause all the crimes. I guess they are too intellectually superior to figure that one out.

I was studying Brian Greene's "Entangling Space," chapter 4 of The Fabric of the Cosmos in class the other day. This entanglement of space came to mind from talking to "Joey" about doing time.

Marcus: So are you done or do you think you'll come back?

Joey: Come on? Do you really have to ask me that? What do you think?

Quantum mechanics and probability. Space and non-locality. What is time? What is space? They don't exist, yet the illusions persist as I listen to Christina Aguilera's "Liberation," and how she's looking for "Maria." Newton's cosmic clock with Einstein's updates explains how the world doesn't work. So why should my literature fit into your framework?

Ever see three basers[2] try to buy one sack with chicken? I did. Right after reading a "Pearl of Wisdom" telling me that all the striving of my love in life and the fulfillment of my mission with mankind is to bring the awareness of God, the I AM that I AM, to them. Meaning we are all foci of the one and same consciousness of whatever you decide to call that light. How do I do that from prison?

I've read so many times over the years that when we incarnate, we lose our memory of higher planes and that we come as teams

---

[1] The mass incarcerated in the State of Florida have to serve 85% of their sentences. Since President Donald Trump has signed a law reducing Federal prison sentences to 71%, the heavily Republican State of Florida is considering reducing its prisoners' sentences to 65-71% for non-violent drug offenses. In Florida's Congress, they are arguing that people with violent crimes and minimum mandatory sentences should not receive relief from the burden of

to bring life, light, and enlightenment to darkened worlds; teams of angels to help planets and their inhabitants. I can feel Christina trying to break the mold of the darkness of the carnal mind to do her duty.

As Americans, we have a duty to the world and its species. We have the money, technology, and freedom to push our race/species to higher levels. But we get afraid to express our beliefs and ideas for fear of upsetting the herd. When did we become animals? The Goddess of Liberty holds up a flame in Manhattan not a piece of meat. When did we stop identifying with light?

Bruce Lee realized that light. Racial pride divides us and is the cause of most discord in civilization. If we all came to the common knowledge of us being light, stars in flesh, maybe the hatred would slowly subside. Aren't we the stars and stripes? Is this not why we were given power? Not to gloat and flaunt, but to uplift and strengthen by that light shining through us in all its glory.

Maybe it expresses through Christina in song and James Ryan through building engines. That brilliance shines regardless, but I'd be letting Siddhartha Gautama Buddha down by not pointing

---

bearing the lengthy sentences, even though the criminal code is racist and outdated and was formatted to continue the institution of slavery. Two bills for prison reform and reduction of sentences were struck down and voted against in Florida's legislature last year, which would have brought relief by reducing the lengths of sentences, but only for non-violent drug offenders.

[2] A "baser" is American street slang for a "drug addict." A "sack" is a small, packaged amount of whatever drug the addict is seeking to use. Three of these drug addicts were jostling to be the first to purchase one sack like it was a Northern Pacific stock certificate in the corner of 1901. These three addicts were using chicken sandwiches as currency to buy the sack because they didn't have cash or credit.

it out. Jesus Christ said to let your light shine for the world to see, and "that when they hate you for it, understand they hated me first."

So, our adversaries in Russia, Iran, and the like call Americans "Satanic Devils" and "the head of the snake." While lusting after everything we've worked, killed, sacrificed, argued, nurtured, slaved, and died to build. God bless the military. Without which this insensitive, disrespectful, and completely oblivious Ivy League professor at Princeton wouldn't have the protection to devise thoughts on the equality of humans and animals. Concluding from the brilliance of his logic that a poodle is no different than an orphan in our over-crowded foster care system due to the opioid epidemic. As if our precious babies are just puppies in the pound.

I'm lit, and the liberty flame burns brightly in me because of love. Love for the fools at Princeton programmed like an academic religious cult that is indoctrinated by his papers. "They know not what they do." When this uncivil discourse and highly inflammatory language reaches this level of living outside those ivory towers, We, The People, have compassion for this ignorance.

There's a freedom and honesty that comes from Joey knowing he's coming back to prison after living fast and enjoying his time smoking crack with beautiful fast women. Not much different than listening to a song on repeat. It's his cycle, his Karma. I don't judge. I'm here with y'all. We reflect each other and sometimes we see things we don't like and try to change it.

I don't know where I'm going with this, but it's hard. It's hard being in prison. It's hard being alone. It's hard overcoming lower nature and human form, taming and killing the beast. It's hard being a man, no matter how easy the media makes it seem. I can't complain about coming back to my bunk from a day of modern slave labor and not having a woman to talk to or beer to drink. I have to "man up." Suck it up. Be a man. Meaning, don't have feelings. Pretend you don't need a woman's love.

"You are a worthless criminal. You should have thought about that before you shot your music promoter. Inmate! You are no longer a citizen. Inmate! Cut your hair! Shave your face! Get naked, squat, and cough! Cuff up! Inmate!"

I'm surrounded by hatred and mean mugs. Cut throats and swindlers. Kindness is shocking. A myth . . . in here, but as I awaken to non-locality, what I know as oneness, the earth becomes the stage, stadium, court, and field where we perform in this play, concert, game, and war . . .

What are we fighting for? Why do we perform? What are we competing for? What's the prize?

Attention?

Is that the goal? How much attention do we really want or need? Who creates our thoughts? Do we create from the heart anymore? Are we a bunch of mimics?

Absolutes are what I've sought since I was fourteen. I'm thirty-six as of the date of this writing and have learned a lot from Saint Germain. So, I believe in kindness, love, mercy, diplomacy, and justice. Not everybody can be the villain in the movie, so I chose to side with the ones who are dedicated to beauty and perfection . . . in the eye of the beholder. Building heaven on earth together even when we gotta go through hell or destroy it. I live to love and nothing else. Even when no one loves me. I just listen to Christina and remember . . .

INTRODUCTION 2 REBEL OF DA UNDERGROUND

"Da Chronicles of Kamal (Time Prevails)" *Book of Symbols^

Will

A rebel, face 2 face wit da devil,
Hell in his community.
Tired of viewing drug use and
Eulogies, supernatural
Powers influence poetry.
Intellect 2 da 3rd degree,
Reside in his mind if u care.
2 witnesses, da destruction of
A mad chemist,
breeding Consequence like viruses,
Resurrecting Osiris Hieroglyphs.
Rebel's a hero, maybe a villain
Depending on wat uniform u
Fit in. Nana dealt wit marches
And sit-ins.
Rebel neva
Stands alone,
infatuated by cultural
Representation on da microphone.
Exchanging his soul 2 breathe life in people,
some view it evil.
If he starred in film,
may not survive
a sequel;
but would u root for him 2 defeat
Da darkness that plagues his kingdom?
Dis young prince, not 2 eloquent
most of his partners got felonies.
Childhood crush remains celibate

Hoping he won't 4get da dream,
the resurrection of a newborn King.

yellow(s)

\ ye-(ˌ)lō \ — *noun*

> yellowness (the chromatic color resembling the hue of
> sunflowers or ripe lemons)

\ ye-(ˌ)lō \ — *adjective*

> yellowish (of the color intermediate between green and orange
> in the color spectrum); easily frightened; sensationalistic;
> jaundiced; changed to a yellowish color by age

\ ye-(ˌ)lō \ — *verb*

> turn yellow

HOME IN MEMORY

Roger

On Mother's Day, I smell lighter fluid wafting through the window from the Warden's house just beyond the fences and into my nostrils. I'm lying on my bunk during count as the scent of burning charcoal takes me back to childhood when such a scent was very near and very nearly an every-weekend affair. The sound of Alabama in my ears, "There's no way I could make it without you . . ." completes the transformation from lost to found . . .

Dad and uncle Randall are at the table talking about the new Diamond Rio trucks they are driving at the company and how the front pour is much easier; Uncle James, uncle Robbie, and Grandpa are on the porch talking about grouper and how best to clean and cook them; Mom, aunt Julie, aunt Sandra, and Grandmother are at the grill talking about the Tupperware they just purchased and how convenient it is that all the lids are interchangeable; Grandma, aunt Red, and Aimee are at the pool talking about dad, Randall, Sandra, and James when they were kids. Mom tells me I'm spoiling my dinner that's cooking on the grill by eating potato chips. But they're sour cream, my favorite kind! I grab another handful.

"Happy Mother's Day, mom!" I say as I cram the handful of chips in my mouth and hug her.

"Thank you! I love you," she says.

"I love you too," I let go and run off to find my cousin, Michael, as she yells after me, "Don't go far, dinner will be ready soon!"

Michael's laying on a bean bag chair watching something on television. He's about to turn thirteen in three weeks. I'll be a teenager too, in two more years. I grab my new Debbie Gibson cassette tape, put it in the cassette deck, and push "play." "Oooooh only in my dreeeeeams. As real as it may seeeeem. It was only in my dreeeeeaam,"starts playing. They play this song all the time at Melody Skating Rink. "I wonder when they'll have another all-night skate?" I ask out loud. Michael says probably once the summer starts. Two more weeks of school until summer! I tell him, "Come on, let's go ride!"

Strings tied to our bicycle seat posts, Tonka trucks follow our every slide, skid, and jump over the little hills we exaggerate into jumps as we peddle furiously down the sugary sand road to Shawn's house. He's out in the front yard and sees us coming. He walks over to his bike, picks it up, and jumps on. He meets us halfway down his driveway and I say, "Hey. What's up?"

"Hey," he says and asks if we're BBQing.

"Yeah, we gotta get back soon to crank the handle on the homemade peach ice cream." Man, I'm glad they all agreed to peach instead of chocolate, but vanilla would've been good, too, with the pecan pie. He shows me his new pegs on the back of his bike. I say, "Cool." Then he shows me his new hat pins. One is two rifles crossed in the middle and the other is a gold bald eagle with white feathers on its head.

"A dollar apiece," he tells me.

"Awesome!" I say. He always finds the best deals and all the best hat pins at the flea market. Michael is ready to go, and I wave and yell, "Come down later if you can!" as we spin out down his mulch driveway pulling the trucks on strings.

Mom and dad are calling me to get my hands washed and to

grab a plate. And it's my turn to churn the ice cream. I am hungry no matter what mom said about the chips. I love this place.

Uncle Randall tongs a burger onto my plate as a tear forms in my eye from the smoke of the grill. But suddenly I realize it's not from the smoke, only the memory, as I realize how lost and far from home I am.

"What's your number, inmate?! This isn't time to daydream," an officer standing outside my room door exclaims, and I'm jerked back completely to the here and now.

"9630891, sir," I respond by rote. I sigh and wipe my eye.

NEW YEAR'S EVE

John K.

One dark grey winter afternoon
I hang a birdfeeder in a leafless tree
   seeds spilling onto the snow as I turn it this way and that
      —looking for the perfect angle—
     already fretful at the waste.

Old doubts are never far from my tattered heart:
   What if nothing finds it, have I got the right seeds
     (and those squirrels, stealing what wasn't meant for them,
    bold as sin—shouldn't they eat as well?)
   And cardinals! I crave that lightning-flash of crimson
     cutting clean across these bare and heartless heights—
  But last year there were only wrens, dowager-drab
    and dim as dusk's last light.

I trudge up the steps and wonder why I bother
   as I shed the last layers that shield me from the cold.
Nestled fireside in an old comfortable chair,
   glancing out my living-room window I can see it, vacant now,
    a modest monument to folly so late in the year.

And doesn't kindness sometimes seem to wear you down,
   the little gambles you take when you've lost too many bold bets,
     backing away, broken again by the sirens' sweet assurance:
       Happiness is over here, over here.
Near sun-up I will take my seat—let this glass be clear—
   Who knows what flutter and feast first light may bring,
      The fleeting joy of bright-hued voices as they sing.

THE GRASS

Pete

We lived on a corner lot in a semi-rural area and, to put it bluntly, there was a lot of grass. In the summer the grass wanted to grow faster, and I had two boats in the yard. Can you see my problem? The boats wanted my attention whereas the grass demanded it. Have you been faced with your own wants versus needs scenario? Who won yours? The wants, right? Yeah, we're all probably the same. It's hard to argue with logic, so much easier to ignore it.

I began prioritizing areas of the yard that needed the most attention in order to get water time. To me, this made all the sense in the world; to my wife Karen, that was another story. She kept getting on me about the yard looking "patched up" as I would mow just the front yard, next time it would be part of the back over the drain fields, or the side yard that was on a slope down to the road. Now understand, I am only doing one part at a time, so they are all in different stages of growth. So, it did look ragged, but we were out on the water most every weekend.

One weekend I'm out back mowing away when a lawn service truck turned around the corner. I flagged down the driver and received an estimate on mowing my yard. When he left, another lawn service team passed by, and I received another estimate. They say third time's a charm; well, it was. The third truck pulling a trailer came around the corner and, being a pro by now, I flagged down the driver. He said that if I could convince one of my neighbors to also hire his company to mow our yards at the same time, he would do it for this price, and showed me an estimate. I pulled out both of the other business cards and for two yards, his estimate was better than both of the first two lawn companies.

You know that I was done mowing grass for the day. I hired him on the spot for that monthly charge and he told his crew to take care of both yards. These guys start unloading the trailer, and they have this big-ass lawnmower with car tires on it and wings that unfold, which gave about a twelve-foot-wide mowing area. I put my mower back in the shed, and the boss and I stood in the shade to drink a cold beer. His crew swarmed over the two yards finishing in record time. These guys didn't miss anything before packing the trailer as fast as they unloaded it. I gave them all a beer before they were off to assault the next patch of overgrown grass.

When Karen came home, fully expecting to see me not mowing but also not finished, she was pleasantly surprised to see everything looking so neat as the house came into view. I was sitting out back looking the part with a sweaty t-shirt and grassy clothes as she joined me to comment on how well the yard looked. As we sat there, she kept studying the tracks going across our yard. She leaned forward to look around the edge of the house only to see all these tire tracks six feet apart going right up into our neighbor Rachael's yard. Now compare what she was seeing with my standard lawnmower, which is about three feet wide and has one and a half to two-inch-wide tires.

Karen is a smart woman, and I knew that she knew that the husband she left mowing the yard was not, in fact, the mower of her grass and that, being the smart wife that she was, it didn't matter to her in the long run because her yard was not patched up but actually looking pretty spiffy. That was Saturday. Guess where we were on Sunday?

PONTOON BOAT HELL

Pete

One beautiful, sunny Sunday my wife Karen, our friend Mike, and myself went out on the Indian River in South Brevard County on our 26-foot pontoon boat, a SunTracker Party Barge. We launched on the West side of the Indian River at the Grant, Florida boat ramps and made our way South down the river and then to the East side where the Sebastian Inlet cuts through the barrier island.

The day was spent swimming in the inlet, diving in the crystal-clear water, and simply enjoying a beautiful Florida summer day. We anchored in the river just to the North of the inlet because there were no houses or Mangroves covering the shoreline. Neither were there docks or landing areas along the Western shoreline of the barrier islands at that spot, and by dropping the anchor we were sure the boat would be there when we came back up out of the water. The river is mainly a brackish water, meaning it's fresh and saltwater mixed and not clear. Just inside the inlet, though, it is predominantly saltwater and crystal-clear down to its 30-foot depth.

Around early afternoon, we noticed black clouds way North up the river that we guessed to be around the Titusville area. As the day was bright, sunny, and warm, with no clouds in the sky where we were, what was happening in Titusville was of no concern. Sometime later, one cool gust blew across our boat. We all looked North and saw the black clouds were at the Cocoa area. This was a fast-moving summer storm, and we were far away from any protective structures.

We started packing things away to start the short distance back

North to Grant, which unfortunately was on the other side of this wide river. No sooner did we get underway than the wind picked up, blowing almost horizontally, bringing with it rain. This was the type of storm that, if experienced from inside a house, would buffet the windows with hard gusts of wind-driven rain. A person looking out the windows of a house would see sheets of water blowing across the yard instead of simply falling from the sky as rain normally does.

The pontoon boat had a hard top that hinges forward to lay on the short side walls along the edge of the forward deck. I asked Mike to take the helm so that I could release the pins securing the top in the upright position. Once it was released and hinged down forward on the rails it would not stay. The wind gusts were hard and constantly trying to rip the top out of my grip. With my feet planted against each side of that little aluminum wall that's around the deck, I was doing a split never thought possible. I pulled down three of the fifteen life preservers hanging from the underside of the hardtop and passed two back and quickly wiggled into mine while not letting go of the top.

Karen knew then that things weren't going well, even though I had blocked her and Mike from the blunt force of the storm when I brought the hard top down to rest on the hard sides effectively creating a cocoon for them. Although life preservers for flotation are required by the Coast Guard, I had never donned one in all our boat outings together.

By now the boat was in the middle channel of a river that's approximately one and a half miles wide in that area. There was a storm raging out of the North right into my face as I stood legs spread wide, trying desperately to weigh more, while pulling down on the leading edge of our roof with everything I owned. The wind tried unceasingly to possess the top part of our boat. I started screaming at Mike to take us back to shore because it was painfully evident that Grant, which was to the North, was not attainable as there was a great possibility we may not have been moving forward at all. The pontoon boat was a leisurely cruiser, not a power boat.

Mike was screaming just as loud that he had to keep it facing the wind. When in a storm involving high winds or high waves, while in a boat, there are few lifesaving rules. One of them is keep the bow pointed into the storm lest you be capsized. I knew he was right, but in my defense the storm had me scared spitless, and, no, I don't think that is a word. I screamed, "It's my boat; take us to shore!!!" This exchange went back and forth until Mike, against his better judgment, turned it ever so slightly West towards the mainland—and the wind got under us. The full fury of the storm blasted the right hand, starboard side, and wedged under that 26' pontoon made of round, practically weightless, aluminum. The wind tilted the boat up on the left hand, port side pontoon before proceeding to skip and skim it Southwest across the river letting us go when the rising shoreline blunted its strength. The whole flight seemed to take less time than it just took to describe.

The river was shallow a good distance from the West shore in this area, so docks extended quite a way out from the mainland. Our uncontrollable travel ended mere feet from the end of one of these docks. There was a dock pylon within reach at the left front pontoon when the wind set us down. I jumped out from under the top I was holding to grab it in a death grip. This represented something anchored to Mother Earth and, right about then, I needed something that wasn't going to move. Mike powered the boat around until it would have the wind at our back and started all over convincing me to let go of the dock. It was with reluctance that I did because at that time the feeling of being so close to death was in my throat.

Mike steered the boat around a piece of land that jutted out into the river with a two-story restaurant perched on it. We pulled into some condo's docks immediately to the South of the restaurant and tied off only to look over and see two stories of floor to ceiling glass windows showing tables of diners looking down upon three soaking wet boaters. We had plenty of wet beach towels now, so we hung them all under the top to give a micron of privacy from our shame.

I still love the water and cannot wait to get back on her.

JALERI

Ben

Her father goes away, she's alone and afraid;
He was her best friend, someone she'd confided in.
Captured for breaking laws; should've quit.
The system has failed him; he refused to submit.
She knows he gave her all he had,
Every damn penny down to his last.
She misses the phone calls and the visits,
As well as her father's loving, soft kisses.

Sitting in a cell thinking to himself,
"How in the hell did I get in this mess?"
Judgment on a man born condemned;
The color of his skin makes him guilty, freedom slim.
With little money and no paid attorney,
His fate is left to public pretenders, considered defenders.

Five years, too young to be without;
Her father is all she thinks about.
She tells herself he'll return soon,
While counting cows jumping moon.
Standing 36 inches tall at this time,
Yet her age does not represent her mind.
A tear caresses the side of her cheek;
She cries, begging for some much-needed sleep.
Dreams of good times throughout the night;
She hopes and prays these wrongs be right.

Thirty years' prison time lay on the table,
He bargains, trying to remain humble and mentally stable.

He's offered 17 years, a ridiculous plea deal;
Told the officer he didn't want his lunch meal.
Trying to figure out what to do,
He had to accept what he knew to be true.
But how could he leave his little queen?
He thought, "Do these people know what this really means?"
Sending a father away from his daughter for so long,
"How could this be payment for doing wrong?"

Being separated from someone he loves becomes unbearable;
His life should have been productive, lawful and charitable.
He didn't want to miss her first day of school;
This separation is unjust and cruel.
Incarceration must be a dream.
Reading the Bible is important now,
Praying silently, making vows.
Oh, what a lesson,
Oh, what a blessing,
God shed light on his situation.

She's assisted in writing a letter to him;
He receives it unexpectedly; never had she written anything.
He pictures her little hands clasping a pen,
Smiling as she's writing daddy, her only best friend.
A weekend visitation she gets;
The first time she'd get her soft loving kiss.
He holds her dearly,
Not wanting to let her go, ever.
They talk, they vibe,
They smile, they laugh, they cry.
They share a beautiful bond.

Her hair has grown longer, a soft brown color.
She smiles, missing two front teeth.
She talks with confidence and concern;
He responds the same in return.
Sentenced to 17 years, freedom far like the moon;

His mission now, is getting out soon.
Education is essential;
Maturing is beneficial.

Being separated from someone he loves
Compels him to understand the actions of self,
The how's, the whys.
His responsibility as a father is enhanced,
Because he now sees he has a chance
To make something out of this
Life that he's been blessed with.

She's stands at his shoulders now,
Having grown two feet in five years, wow.
His little queen notices the changes in him,
From his letters and conversations.
Her mother is astonished by the elevation,
Didn't see or expect the transformation.
She knows her daddy is destined for greatness,
So she sits back and waits with patience.
Freedom is valuable;
Family love is irreplaceable.

ALL-AMERICAN

Marcus

Beyoncé said, "Pretty hurts." So does time.
Paid the toll, gave up my soul to get this Golden Mind.
Dead sleep. Didn't know that I was holding iron.
Soft core stimulated fiber optic lines.
Pulling Strings.
From where we rule our dreams.
One Nation Under God; we are the Kings and Queens.
Broad stripes, bright stars.
Loud bikes, fast cars.
New hope, machine guns "you'll remember me."
Dallas, Texas between Florida and Tennessee.
Tap-tap-tap.
Yeah, I'm listening.
Who is Allen White?
My name is Marcus _____.
I've never been to London.
You must think I'm him or somethin',
and what's a bit coin?
Master Card and cash . . .that's all I know.
So either take me in, or let me go.
What you used to work for. Preet. Mr. Bahara?
Brahma, Vishnu, Shiva . . .Ma Matta Ma Matta.
And you can tell him that.
But you can't tell I'm black because I'm blended in.
Cherokee, French, Irish, Scot, Sioux, and Mexican.
Oroku Saki . . .Feel like a kid again.
Now who gone stop me I'm All-A
I'm All-A
I'm All-American.

AL AÑO VIEJO
31 de diciembre de 2013

Antonio

Pronto mueres—¡Ay! ¡Cómo lo siento! —
    y está medio mundo festejando,
    de tu presencia ya olvidando,
mientras, gravísimo, pierdes aliento,
su calor hecho un frío viento.
    Mas a tu lado prefiero estar
    y tus consejos rememorar:
Me encontraste solo y triste,
mas olvidar y seguir pudiste
enseñarme. Despertar hiciste

Mi corazón con tus lecciones:
Que, siendo corta esta vida,
—Entre dos noches un breve día —
cada cual tendrá ocasiones
que probarán sus convicciones;
Que la vida en el presente
se vive: No con insolente
mirada a un pasado
que es considerado
sobre su justo grado;

Que llegan y se van amores
con impetuosa marejada,
dejando en su estela a cada
uno su porción: Aquí dolores,
allí los sentimientos mejores
que del alma pueden emanar.
¡Oh! ¡Cómo se suele amainar

el sufrimiento con reflexión
sobre un beso, una canción
o de una dulce voz el son;

Que tus estaciones bien figuran
todos mis días en miniatura.
Primavera: Infancia pura.
Las flores con sol y lluvia maduran,
Y el niño con alimento. Mudan
    ambas. Adolescencia y verano
caminan mano a mano:
Como los días se alargan,
así las facultades ensalzan
y su auge pronto alcanzan.

Tu otoño es decadencia
en un cuerpo ya adulto,
que lleva en su bulto
problemas, enfermedad, creencia
—La pesa que asume la existencia.
Es en plenitud de invierno,
la vejez, que yaces tierno:
Tu estertor me da mal agüero.
Contigo siento que me muero.
¡Escucha! Llega el año nuevo.

¡Aguanta un poco más!
Aún nos queda un minuto.
¡No te hagas el difunto!
¿Para dónde es que te vas?
¿Desde allá verme podrás?
¿Nos volveremos a ver?
¿En paraíso o tras renacer?
¿En otro universo? ¡Despierta!
Ya pasó del umbral de la puerta
El nuevo año. ¡Despierta! ¡Despierta!

green(s)

\ grēn \ — *noun*

greenness (resembling the color of growing grass); green park, commons; greens, leafy vegetable

\ grēn \ — *adjective*

greenish (of the color between blue and yellow in the color spectrum); unripe, immature;

\ grēn \ — *verb*

turn or become green "The trees are greening"

AFRAID TO BE ME

David

I am a fifty-year-old gay male. This is no significant deal in today's society; however, I grew up in the 80's. Back then it was not kosher to be open about your sexuality. There have been amazing changes over the past couple of decades that, at times, I find overwhelming.

I come from a small family that at one time was very conservative. Thus, having a gay son back then more than likely would not have been accepted. We moved around a lot as well. I spent my elementary school years in Salisbury, Maryland; middle and early high school years in Tampa, Florida; later high school years in St. Louis, Missouri. I was smallish for my age, had poor eyesight, and was non-athletic. Thus, I got teased a lot. Being openly gay would have just added to the teasing. By the age of twelve I knew I liked boys and not girls.

In Tampa I obtained my first part-time job at the age of fourteen. This is where I met my first partner who I'll call Mark for the story. Mark was nineteen or twenty and in college. Back then his age was not an issue. However, he hid his sexuality from his family as well. Mark taught me all I know about sex. With Mark, we were more friends than lovers. We enjoyed each other's company. He was always polite and never forced me to do anything I did not want to do.

When my folks were out of town, Mark would take me to parties on his college campus. He always introduced me as his younger cousin. His friends tried their best to out-drink me, yet, most failed since I'd been drinking for a year. I was quickly accepted in their college culture. They also introduced me to great music as well--Pink Floyd, The Doors, Depeche Mode, and the like.

When we moved to St. Louis I was super depressed and purposefully did poorly in school. School was not easy, but I was an average student. In St. Louis I met Bryan. Even though Bryan was a freshman, we got along well and had a lot in common, like music and food. We became partners. The other kids in school knew. Teens here were more open about their sexuality than in the South, at least at school and with friends. Bryan was good for me as he was not a drinker nor a drug user. Having Bryan made my life easier as we could hang out together and not be questioned. When I wanted some alone time with him I could have him sleep over. With Mark we had to be careful how we acted in public as being openly gay was not all that accepted in the South. Around his friends I was always his cousin to keep the straight persona alive. That made me feel not wanted at times, yet Mark always made up for this when we were alone and could have our private time. But with Bryan we could be free to express our feelings towards each other at school and amongst peers. We were into going to the mall and movies. By then I had my first car, which was a 1981 Toyota Celica Coupe.

While growing up, my partners were considered to be "friends from school." Upon my graduation from high school in 1988 I moved back to Florida. I was away from my folks but still lived with family. Now my partners were "co-workers," and when I moved out, they were "roommates." My partners would be invited to family meals, and thus we had to keep the straight persona.

It was not until the age of twenty-eight, out of spite during an argument, that I openly told my folks I was gay. At first this caused tremendous friction between me and my father. We did not even speak to one another for over a year. At this point the only other people who knew were my sister and a cousin from New Jersey.

I did not get arrested until I was thirty-five and arrived at prison at the age of thirty-seven. At first, I did my best to hide my true self and attempted to be "normal." It was not until a couple of years ago that a friend harassed and teased me until I felt good about being me. This usually occurred at mealtime. One day, as he told one of his jokes, I busted out laughing. Then I realized the joke was directed at me. It was a great burden that had been released by not having to care anymore. Now I am open, and I do not give a shit what others think of me. For the first time in my life, I have other gay friends. I now read gay literature and magazines. I have known my current partner for over ten years. Sadly, we are at different camps. My father and I have never been closer than we are now. My father encourages me in my pursuit of higher education, which helps me to focus on my goals of completing college and culinary school. My father wants me to be happy in life, even if he is not in total agreement.

Being gay today is far more acceptable than it was when I was growing up. There are many amazing support groups. Plus, you now have the opportunity to marry your partner. The LGBTQ community is something I embrace and no longer hide from. At the age of fifty I can honestly say I am no longer afraid to be me. My advice to those struggling to tell their families is to find a good online support group to help with questions and concerns. We in the LGBTQ family are not alone. But learn from my mistakes; it is better to open up to your family in a positive setting and not during an argument out of spite.

Be proud to be you!

ALCHEMY

Niko

Amor existe para darle vida a la insipidez.
Trust harbors grace in relationships.
Amor no entiende el abandono.
Trust diminishes doubt, becoming beautifully fertile.
Amor supera el egoísmo.
Trust makes longevity feasible.
Amor se concibe a través de la lealtad.
Trust is where reliability is sought.
Amor fortalece esperanza.
Trust repeatedly expresses selflessness like a mantra.
Amor proporciona felicidad en abundancia.
Trust gives one's conscience freedom.
Cuando estos uniquely amazing catalysts se combinan,
What is created es una maravilla.
An Alchemy que da vida a la vida.

THE LIFE OF JOHN
(Against all Odds - A Child Reborn and Emancipated)

Greg

Not too long ago, I heard a story of a teenage boy who was proven to be a menace to his community and society as a whole. His story began in horrific circumstances and, under the right structure, he has become a story of success.

John was raised in a very abusive lifestyle. Many people in the United States are raised in abusive homes. In most scenarios, these people suffer from physical, psychological, or sexual abuses. Those raised in homes that suffer from one of these exploitations may suffer from multiple atrocities. It is not as common for a child to suffer from all three of these abuses simultaneously. Those children that do, typically find themselves restricted to mental hospitals or prisons and, even worse, very early deaths. John was one of those unfortunate children.

From around the age of five-years old he had already suffered from all three abuses from his mother and several men that called themselves stepfathers. John's mother dated the vice-president of the local Hell's Angels biker gang. The Hell's Angels was a notorious and vicious gang in the 1970s. At the end of the school day, when young children were going home to loving families, John's family welcomed him into the Hell's Angels clubhouse. John was passing into a realm so violent that he would literally shake with terror. At any given time, the activities inside the clubhouse would range from heavy drug and alcohol abuse, open sexual activities, and severe physical altercations where knives and guns were always used. At the age of around seven- or eight- years old, while John was playing a game of pool inside the clubhouse, his mother was physically attacked by a gang member. John rushed to her aid but was pushed violently to the floor. A moment later, his mother's boyfriend arrived, and he beat the other member with brass knuckles until he was lifeless. He then violently beat John for not finding a weapon to defend his mother. It was events like this that molded a layer of hatred, heavier drug abuse, and sexual immorality around John. He was becoming a product of his environment.

Unfortunately, John was addicted to drugs by seven-years old. His mother blew "shot-guns" of marijuana smoke into his face and laced his bottles with alcohol as an infant. She initially started infusing him with these substances to keep him quiet and, as he developed, for entertainment—to watch little John act crazy. John says that he would dance wildly and, when certain songs played on the stereo, he would bang his head on the wall until he was almost unconscious. He noticed he was different from the other kids in elementary school. A typical day would start well for John, but by mid-day he became irritable. He suffered through the remainder of the school day and, once home, was able to get high with his mother. His irritability was immediately gone, and he enjoyed the rest of the day with other neighborhood kids. They would arrange furniture that was abandoned on the side of the roads to build make-shift ramps and then use their bicycles to perform stunts while pretending to be Evil Knievel. A lot of skin and blood was lost due to wiping out.

By the time John was seven-years old he was placed into foster care because of an incident that occurred after he was found playing "house" with a neighborhood girl that was the same age. They were holding each other as if they were married when his mother walked in. She ran the little girl away and proceeded to beat John and she hurled him off a second-story balcony. He was in and out of foster homes because of the abuses that he suffered at the hands of his family. Some of these atrocities were physical violence that could be defined as sadistic: being deprived of food, drug abuse, and lascivious exploitations that he suffered at the hands of his mother and other members of his family. Except for his grandmother, he trusted no adults in his family because they abused his small body. He witnessed gang violence in the streets that can only be compared to horror movies. If the events were written here, most readers would wonder whether or not they were fact or fiction.

I can assure you that these atrocities are true and recorded in way of police reports, Department of Child Services Reports, Psychological Reports, and eyewitnesses. In brief and very censored, they range from gang leaders being beheaded, gun fights, multiple murders, and unimaginable savageries. John explains the terror that he felt in many of these events. He recalls hearing and lightly feeling a whistling bullet pass his ear during a shoot-out. He curled into a ball under a pile of garbage and cardboard boxes trying to make himself invisible to the violence that was going on all around him. When John did not hear anymore gunfire, only the faint sounds of police sirens, he jumped up and ran with all of his might to the other side of town, into his grandmother's safe arms. He felt her safe, warm embrace but couldn't talk about what he experienced.

By the time that John was thirteen-years old he was essentially living on his own. Some of his relatives tried to intervene, but their lifestyles did not offer John a different paradigm. He was continuously subjected to drugs, violence, and sexual immorality by family members. The exception was John's grandmother. She was the love of his life. Unfortunately, she was unaware of the way John was being raised and treated. His grandmother knew she was being lied to when she tried to figure out why he seemed to be afraid. She noticed that John would pull or jerk away if there was unexpected or fast movement around him. He would run into his grandmother's bedroom and sit on the floor next to her bed, furthest from the door with his legs pressed to his chest in a ball, shaking with fear. She would hold and love him, unlike other adults in his life. His grandmother was the only adult he trusted. The only thing she could do was allow John to stay with her as often as possible.

John spent most of his life in the streets of the big city. He thought that he had the world by the tail, but destiny had him by the throat. When he was twelve or thirteen-years old, his daily life consisted of heavy drug use: injecting cocaine mixed with heroine and on occasion with gun powder, psychedelic drugs, smoking and/or sniffing cocaine, and heavy amounts of alcohol. John survived financially by making money anyway the streets made possible. John skipped school one day and hung out with several street bums. They purchased several pints of Wild Irish Rose and after excessive drinking, blacked out. Walking the streets, totally unaware of anything, they went into McDonalds. Witnesses state that John was arguing with an adult and he pulled out his revolver-pellet gun from his book bag when several people tried to grab him. Kicking and wildly thrashing to try and get away, he struck several people including a pregnant woman. John managed to free himself and fled, but eventually others jumped on him and restrained him until the police arrived. He was given medical attention and they found that his blood/alcohol level was so high that the doctors were astonished that he was not dead. He was booked into the County Jail for the first time. John was sent to a couple of psychiatrists and both of them recommended that he be placed into immediate care, that he was dealing with extreme anger issues resulting from family cruelties. John fell through the cracks of the system, never to receive any professional help, and he spiraled out of control.

By the time John was sixteen-years old he was zombie-like, with the sole purpose of finding ways to stay high. He was angry at the world and not sure why, completely and utterly lost. John was unaided, birthed from drugs and violence, and was living an illusory life. It was during this time that he lost his mind and broke down. He committed a violent murder accompanied with other charges, was found guilty, and sent to prison for life.

While in prison, John found a new world that provided multiple roads that he could travel. As in society, they varied from gangs, drugs, violence, and a new term called "reform." In the early part of his incarceration, John was living as he was in society: utilizing drugs and living in violence. This was certainly the road most traveled in prison versus the minority that chose reform. But with the concern from a few men in prison and outside volunteers within the system trying to assist inmates, John began to see that he did not have to settle for what he had become. There was a Catholic priest that was instrumental in mentoring John. When John looked into the mirror, he was horrified at what he was. He saw a young man that was ugly from the inside out. If he was ever released from prison, he had no clue how he was going to support and nurture his daughter except to sell drugs, and that was no longer an option. He was functionally illiterate or what he refers to as "dumb as a box of rocks." He was still unable to fully decipher right and wrong. He needed a full transformation.

This was his beginning, a new birth. This change did not come easy for John, because the prison system doesn't mandate rehabilitation, and he was serving a life sentence that did not qualify him for certain programming, i.e., vocational and educational classes. Furthermore, many prisons are violent, hostile environments not conducive to rehabilitation. With the help of a couple volunteers, he received much needed counseling that went on for years. He enrolled in school to earn his GED and started some vocational training. He entered into some residential programs—anger management courses, drug abuse classes, relationship and community development, victim awareness, and very specific classes that dealt with the abuses he sustained as a child from his family. He believed in these programs as he experienced the change take place in his life. He became a leader in these communities, assisting others on their journeys of change. He developed a true faith in his higher power and a very healthy relationship with his daughter, wife, and other family members.

John has consistently found ways to help others that are in similar situations in their life for over fifteen years. He continues to teach anger management, small business, and paralegal programs to the prison population.

John yearns for a second chance at life. He wants to give back to society and help other people as he has in prison. He was resentenced on all of his non-homicide charges and has completed all of these sentences except his homicide. Numerous law enforcement officials, former wardens, friends, volunteers, a Circuit Court judge, and some of the most distinguished trauma experts have all agreed that he has been rehabilitated.

John has many stories that he has, unfortunately, had to endure in his life. Somehow, he managed to lift himself and rise out of the burnt ashes of his past. He declares that his higher power assisted, that he has put in the work to become a man of strong moral fiber and integrity, and he has a passion for life.

Our greatest resource is human life, and it deserves our attention for redemption.

TODAY YOU WILL UNDERSTAND

Tywu

Sitting in the corner
Because I just got hit.
Listening to mom and dad yelling
"you won't amount to shit!"
Growing up an abused child
Trying to be strong, but not wild;
Wanting something or someone to blame,
Needing to scream or burst!
There was a point in my life I thought
"I am the worst."
But now things are not the same;
I've decided to put me first.

· · ·

As my eyes start to open
The light begins to shine.
Watching other students,
I can't be left behind.
Even though learning is tough,
and reading is rough,
That won't be enough.
I am so tired of the bluff;
I can't hear mom and dad saying, "you lost your mind."
But how can I ask for help, when I never did?
Being teased and laughed at
when I was a kid.
Now I'm turning my pain into something to gain.
So, who am I?

MY UNEXPECTED BLESSING

Michael

On September 13, 1991 I was arrested and would eventually spend a short period on Florida's death row for felony murder. This means that while I did not actually kill anyone, the jury felt I was complicit enough to warrant the ultimate penalty. I eventually won my appeal and gave my judge the opportunity to correct what for him was "the only death penalty I ever handed down that gave me trouble sleeping at night." Twenty-eight years after my arrest an amazing thing happened. No, I was not suddenly released from durance vile, instead, I was given a sign that I am worthy of life and might someday be graced with the privilege of freedom, to be a human being again. Let me begin with a recent occurrence.

On June 13, 2019, the Thursday before Father's Day, I received a letter from a very unlikely source. My youngest sister, Kelly, who has written me only once in twenty-eight years, wrote to me. I was ecstatic! I climbed up onto my top bunk to read this unexpected surprise, wondering what could possibly move her to this. The letter began; "Dear Brother, the DNA is a match; you are a father in Florida." This came as a tad bit of a surprise. In all of these years I have only been "intimate" on three occasions. Each of these times protection was used. I picked up the letter from where I had dropped it and read further: "...apparently, a former girlfriend lied to you saying the babies had died in a car wreck...I hope you remember her name, because the twins want to know as much as possible about her so they can track her down next." Thunder crashed, lightning struck my heart, and I slumped over, nearly falling from a fairly high top bunk. I remember every single moment I spent with this woman. In my mind, in my heart, she should have been "The One."

At this point I am dizzy, hyperventilating from the shock and joy of reading anything from Kelly, to the even bigger shock of hearing such news. I felt anger at the lies, all the years of mourning on or about May 19th each year; every Father's Day regretting so much lost, hating myself for not being there. You see, their mother, Michelle, on May 19th, had called the jail I was at telling me that when she'd gone into labor she had been alone, and so she had to drive herself to the hospital. As she drove past Seminole Lake Park on Park Blvd. in St. Petersburg, Fla., a drunk driver "T-boned" her car pulling out of the park, running the light, then ran off. We know he was drunk because he was later caught. He was a repeat offender. My son, whose name she told me was Robert, was born dead in a pool of blood on the floorboard of the truck, and my daughter, Krystal Lee, was delivered in the E.R., also dead. We had discussed names previously, and neither of these had been mentioned, but not being present, I had no actual say. That was the whole point, I was not there. I saw it as my fault she had to drive herself. I hated myself. I blamed myself. On the way back to the cellblock, I collapsed to the floor crying; I completely lost control of myself. I was consumed by loss, grief, and shame. The deputy escorting me got the story from me, and I was immediately placed on suicide watch against my will.

She told me she'd wanted to name my son Michael, after me, but her boyfriend/fiancé balked at raising another man's child named after the other man, so, "Robert." I wanted to name my son after my two grandfathers, and I wanted my daughter to have the middle name of Marie, as a nod to a generations-old tradition on my mother's side of the family of naming the first-born daughter by this name.

While I am writing this story, I have to lay my pen down. My handwriting is bad enough normally, but my hands are shaking with rage at the memory. You see, Dale was the "other guy" in our relationship. Shortly before I was arrested Michelle had been with Dale. We'd had a falling out over that one. I knew it was going on but was in denial. I had to face the truth. I spoke to Dale that night and left. After a week or so he, a soldier at Tampa's Joint Task Force, had to leave for a training mission in Georgia. A week or so later, on September 9, 1991, Michelle came over. I was on the phone with a girl from work who had just called. I had been trying to set her up with my roommate but was very attracted to her myself. She had just admonished me for always trying to pawn her off on my roommate and asked why I didn't ask her out myself. My door opens and in walks Michelle acting as if she had every right to do so, as if we'd never broken up. Who knows, maybe I was mistaken. After all I am a guy. In her mind nothing was wrong with her view of reality. Michelle realized immediately that I was talking to a girl and stormed out without a word. Somehow, I felt guilty. I was that stuck on Michelle.

About an hour passed while I wondered if she'd come back. Why would she come back? Did I actually want her to? (Yeah, who was I kidding? I was in love with her.) When she walked in again, it was as if she'd never left, as if it was the first time, as if we were still the same two people who for the past months had spent no more than 6-10 hours apart, waking or sleeping. We didn't discuss the girl on the phone, Dale, or the days apart. We fired up where we'd left off; we needed no outside spark to explode.

All of this was on September 9, 1991; we "made up" completely with plans for "letting Dale down easy" and moving to Ybor City. She would get away from Dale; I would get away from my roommate and soon-to-be co-defendant in the murder I am currently incarcerated for. Two days later, on September 11, she and I were at the restaurant where she worked waiting for her shift to begin when Dale called her at work saying he was coming back early. When Michelle told me this, I could see on her face that all of our plans would come to nothing, although she did not say so and I refused to ask. That was the day we took it a bit fast and loose, careless and crazy for each other, because we knew it would not, could not, last. It was unspoken but we both knew, no matter what we really wanted, our plans were nothing but dust and ashes, soon to be blown away. This, our last day together, was the only time she could have possibly become pregnant. Nine months or so later I was in jail, on the phone with Michelle— yeah, that phone call.

Getting back to the letter...

Kelly went on to tell me that Michael and Mariah, as their adoptive parents named them (purely coincidence), had been searching on a DNA website the last four years for a connection to find their birth parents. Kelly had also been on the website looking for connections when they both got hits on each other. The connection was on our mother's side of the rug, and when Kelly saw the photo they sent her, there was no doubt in her mind who in our family was their connection. I have not yet seen these photos, but everyone says they look like me. Poor kids. She continued to say that my son is a pilot and my daughter is a teacher living in the Netherlands. They had lived in Florida for their early years until moving to Missouri. Their adoptive parents were a bit older than average to be adopting, but since they had already raised a set of twins of their own and would keep the siblings together, they had particularly good credentials.

I should give you a bit of perspective as to my state of mind and the impact that this letter had on me. The previous Tuesday I had written a letter that was basically a pity party. In it I stated that because my bloodline will end with me, what is the point of continuing to bear constant abuse and the swallowing of any vestige of pride or self-respect that might still linger in my soul. Should I have to bear daily disrespect from people? Must I accept the abuse of people who by "chain gang"[1] rules shouldn't so much as raise their eyes to me much less their voices! Why must I stand for the constant scorn from men whose respect and esteem had once meant the world to me, who had once considered me to be the ideal of an honorable man, a "stand-up convict." I have changed my lifestyle and "retired" from gang life. I had grown used to people being honored to meet me, calling me a "Legend in the chain gang.[2] My ego ate that up like popcorn shrimp. The only problem with all of that was I sometimes felt the need to live

---

[1] There are rules in the "chain gang" that say people who are physically weak or have "certain charges" like child molesting or lewd and lascivious exposure, must step aside for men with "real "charges, such as bank robbery or murder. Many gangs will seek these people out and offer protection for exchange of favors or canteen items and even cash in the account of the gang leader. Some become the most dangerous hitmen to compensate for their charges and give them a reputation to protect them in their old age.

[2] Throughout my 30+ years in prisons and jails in five states, I have managed to maintain my integrity and character as a stand–up convict—one who's word is a bond of steel and whose reputation is such that for someone to say "Lockjaw said this," it will be accepted as true, without question. (I am named Lockjaw in the chain-gang.) I am known to not be a snitch and to be fair minded. I will not allow anyone of my people to be disrespected nor will I condone my people to be junkies, thieves, or basically the type of men whose behavior would embarrass us as an organization.

up to the reputation earned as a much younger man who healed a lot faster and was able to duck and dodge better. Back then, if I could not duck and dodge, I did not really care; I would wear the bruises as a badge of honor.

I eventually came to despise the effort required to live up to my "legend" (a persona that did not match the man I knew myself to be), although I had enjoyed the benefits throughout the years. Many people would give me a pass if I did or said the wrong thing, in the sure knowledge that the retribution might not be worth the immediate gratification. I also had the name of someone who could hold water, or see things and never talk about them. I always paid my debts be they of honor or money. If I gave my word it would be kept. As I'd grown older, I found I healed slower. Also, I have a parole date that I need to move closer. I am 11+ years D.R. free and know that basically any D.R. (Disciplinary Report), no matter how petty, would mean I must die in prison. So I walk on eggshells. Ego aside, no human being should be treated like we are every day. People who are physically weak, particularly unattractive, or have charges involving children or sex charges in general, are considered to be second class citizens even to other convicts. They are seen as prey to some men, and not worth defending to most others. Other inmates treat them like many of the C/O's[3] treat all of us, like crap. I would guess that it is to boost their own morale, proving how weak-minded too many of us are. I have learned today to see them as people. What they'd done was beneath contempt, but who they are now is what matters. I realized that for the way I had been treating them, it was I who was beneath contempt and deserved to be scorned.

---

[3] Correctional Officer

It is not that they deserve to be respected for their crimes, but that as human beings they deserve the fundamental rights that all people deserve. I demean myself when I demean others, no matter the reason. I came to see that I had acted this way to rationalize my own anger at personal experiences as a victim of violent physical abuse from my father and sexual abuse from another family member. I had also consoled several of my own family members and friends who were victimized while I was powerless to do anything about it. It had all built up and came to be a burden too heavy to carry. I was ready to lay it down and simply die. I merely had to find a route for my departure from this world that I had come to hate, and besides, who would even care?

Eventually there comes a time when the need to conform to the chain-gang roles just seems so, feh. The only thing holding me here in this world was not the basically unrealistic hope of parole, but the love of my parents and my best friend. My sisters, who had meant the whole world to me as I was growing up feeling forgotten by G-d, had completely forsaken me. I had been told to forget that I have sisters. It was at this time that the Creator of all reminded me that He is in the world and that all is right or will come to be so in His time.

My son is a pilot. My daughter is a schoolteacher. They are free of any negative influence they might have been forced to live through had Michelle kept them or allowed my parents to adopt. They would have grown up with the knowledge that their father is a convicted murderer. They might have had to visit prisons and been humiliated by the searches and scorn of the C/O's. Instead, Alex, as he prefers to be addressed, is currently tracking down his mother and two older siblings before obtaining permission to come to the prison for our first visit, by his own choice. To date we have yet to speak on the phone, due to the delays of the FDOC's[4] bureaucratic policies. I have recently received an address for him and have written to him. He has not yet had time to receive it, much less to answer, but I am waiting and hoping and praying.

I look forward to the day when I am united with my kids and we are given the chance to get to know who we are today and share the parts of our past lives that we are comfortable sharing. I realize we have major differences in our realities and that we must make allowances for living in vastly different worlds. I hope that we may one day be able to share everything no matter how nitty or gritty, as friends and family do. Until the day, I await the days to come with a renewed hope for life.

---

[4] Florida Department of Corrections

REFLECTIONS ON SELF

Antonio

Who am I? That will depend on who you ask. In a cold, businesslike manner, the system will tell you that I am X39788, forty-one years old, male, convicted murderer, and lifer. Since I am a Latino, the system will also add that I have been suspected of being a gang member. Almost twenty-one years of close monitoring of my mail, recorded phone conversations, visits, and daily interactions with the prison population has not substantiated this suspicion. What it will not tell you is the numerous times I have dissuaded young men from joining violent prison gangs, an act that could inspire violence against me. In one instance, I had to remind a young friend that the gang needed him and not vice versa. "You already get respect from everyone because of how you carry yourself and not because of who your friends are," I told him. "If you join them, you will be asked to earn your respect." It was not until earlier this year that the system acknowledged that I am not a gang member. Yet it still insists that it can accurately define who I am.

The system will tell you that I am a depraved criminal whose interactions with the outside world must be tightly controlled. Perhaps this is why I am not allowed to sit next to family members when I see them for visitation. I am deemed capable of inappropriately touching my mother, sisters, nieces, or female friends. My hands must be clearly visible when I take pictures with them. Alternately, I may convince them to smuggle drugs, money, or other contraband. Underlying this distrust is the belief I am bent on breaking rules and subverting the security of the institution when given the opportunity. You must accept this cold, hard fact about me as true because it comes from the studied observations of trained professionals. You ignore it at your own peril.

To those doing time around me, I seem to be several different people all at once. To the inmate population at large, I am presumed to be a violent gang member because we Latinos are infamous for sticking together and for stabbing our enemies. Ironically, this same presumption has both shielded me from violence and preserved me from having to use it. In twenty years, I have not had a single fight.

To those who consider themselves "chain-gang rich"[1] because they are financially supported by their families, I am poor, a peon. While I always have money on my books, I don't spend the $100 weekly limit as they do. I tend to be frugal in my spending, stretching my money to last the entire month. However, those bereft of financial support consider me an elitist because I always have money on my account and often prepare meals with others similarly situated. The truth is that I rarely say "no" when the needy ask for a handout. Motivated by a Bible verse that says, "He who gives to the poor lends to the Lord, and He will repay it," I lend, expecting nothing in return, and give forward what is paid back to me.

Although the Bible has informed my giving in prison, the religious perceive me to be some kind of heathen because I rarely,

---

[1] Although the Florida prison system did away with the chain gang decades ago, it persists in the prison vocabulary as synonym for Florida Department of Corrections.

if ever, visit the chapel or voice religious views. To the non-religious, I seem to follow some unspoken moral code. I lend, not seeking interest in return; I return what I find that does not belong to me, and I point out the positive in a negative situation. To those seeking self-improvement—either mental, spiritual, or physical—I am a fellow traveler on the path of life. I am one who's enduring the same hardships and is learning the same difficult lessons.

To the lazy, I am a workout fanatic, exercising far too much for the meager diet we are served. To my workout partner and a few others, I am dedicated and motivating. I adapt high intensity interval training (HIIT) and CrossFit workouts I read in magazines to the prison environment. The lean and athletic bodies my workout partner and I have achieved have led other exercisers to ask us questions like what exercises they can do to trim fat or to target a specific body part.

To some, I am a nerd because of my glasses, books, and seemingly endless supply of crossword puzzles. I do consider myself a nerd because of my reading interests, manner of speech, and comportment. Sometimes I am seen as a walking encyclopedia. I was definitely such to the young men who turned around during yesterday's evening news and asked me who Rembrandt was.

To my immediate family, I am a tragic figure, an unrelenting cause of sorrow. I am one who had amazing potential but lost it all on the streets. I am a firstborn son among six children. I am the head of a generation who has been irretrievably uprooted from the family tree. I am a stump. I am that one who has been conspicuously absent from all the family functions—birthdays, reunions, vacations, weddings, births, and even funerals—since 1999. I am that older brother whom my brothers and sisters cannot rely on for advice and guidance in times of need. I am that favorite uncle to nieces and nephews who have only known me within the context of a visiting park; who leave wondering why I always wear the same clothes, and why I never leave with them. I am a memory, the shadow of a distant memory, to all but a few out of a very large extended family.

But who am I to myself? I am one who has decided to reject all the labels and stereotypes with which others—the system, the chain-gang, family, and friends—would bind him. I am neither a murderer, nor a depraved criminal, nor a violent gang member, nor a heathen, nor a workout fanatic, nor any other label that would diminish my immensity. I am one who strives to be true to himself without bending to the demands and expectations of others. I am one who has cast aside all the –isms that would constrict his wide worldview to a narrower one. Leaving behind the restricting halls of conformity, I am one who has learned the freedom that individuality brings. I refuse to live like a violent savage simply because I live in a violent place. I refuse to stop learning about myself and the world outside these fences because I may never see that side again. I refuse to escape my reality by abandoning myself to drugs. I am one who has learned that the soul is more immense than these confining walls and razor wire. I am one who seeks his own reasoned answers to the enduring questions of human existence and reality: What is the meaning of life, why are we here, and how should we live?

This is a thirst that no single human authority, no catechism or religious text, no philosophical treatise can slake. In the words of Søren Kierkegaard, "I seek a truth that is true to me." I do not mean a truth that is relative and comfortable for me, but one that penetrates to the core of my being. I am one who thirsts for knowledge. Be it science, the social sciences, literature, or mathematics, I want to know. How does this work? How was that made? Why does that happen? How did we come to this? Who did what? When did that happen?

With these musings, I momentarily transcend this stagnant and putrid environment and free myself from it. In these moments, I cease to be who the system, my fellow prisoners, and my family say that I am. All they say I am becomes distant and irrelevant. In these moments, I am nothing but a living and inquisitive human soul. In these moments, I am myself.

EXCEEDING EXPECTATIONS

Ben

BEFORE

I think I know what I'm doing,
I used to say.
I'm old enough to do what I want.
Only sixteen, without big dreams.
My intention was to survive past twenty-five;
More than a few friends of mine had died.
County jail beds became my resting place,
Bullet wounds became the norm;
A brain with intelligence, yet to be formed.
Drug money provided the necessities;
Two children became
Wholesome responsibilities.
Friends I thought I had,
Misguiding, leading me down wrong paths.
Negative energy absorbed and consumed,
Which led to eight by twelve rooms.
Thinking, "something must change,"
A young man suffering too much pain.
Falling victim to the prison system,
Another so-called black statistic.
Educated by a negative environment,
Blamed for being ignorant.
Judges condemning time and time again;
I must change, I must win!
My life seems worthless;
I keep doing the same thing,
Am I insane?

AFTER

School is where my life begins.
TABE scores show I'm capable,
G.E.D. test scores 'with honors' now able!
Plato says, "never cease from learning,"
Desire for knowledge keeps burning.
Stetson University C.E.P. is offered;
I sign up hoping my admission was proper.
Life seems bright on this path;
Higher education in prison,
I've got a chance to take.
Surprising myself at accomplishments,
Wowed by the elevation in competence!
Family shocked when I speak or write;
My mind has become like
a LED light, 'bright'!
I've cultivated a mission to share
Everything I've learned because I care
Not only about the existence of "self,"
But, also my family's spiritual,
Mental, and financial wealth!
Oh, how blessed I am,
Knowing higher knowledge
Is not just another scam.
I'm a breathing example of
What proper education does—
Empowers and Challenges the labels,
That have been imposed upon me!

MORE THAN MY BLUES

Earl

The journey to my blues started at the age of nine. I was a young boy from a single-parent home because my mom separated from my stepfather. She was left raising five kids while working two jobs. I was left with no father, no positive male figure in my life, and to my own devices. Without a positive adult male figure in my life, I was destined to be sucked into the streets because I was both naïve and curious—a bad recipe.

That recipe produced a young person idealizing the wrong things. On the streets of St. Petersburg, Florida I started to see the "older guys"—teenagers and young adults—kicking it with the girls and I wanted that too, even at the age of nine. I also saw the drug deals going down and the money that the guys on the block were making. I would sneak away from home to go hang out with the guys. My mom did all she could to raise me right and to the best of her ability. I did nothing to help her. I did nothing to show her what she had instilled in me, what she had taught me.

There were times in my life when I would see my friends with their fathers and get jealous and want so badly to have a father in my life, but I was too young to communicate that to anyone. Without that much-needed role model, I started shoplifting from stores like K-Mart, JC Penny, etc. I became so good at it that I began to forget to look for clues that would let me know to walk away, like someone paying close attention to me. As a result, I eventually was caught. Looking back, I know now that the ambiance of the streets of St. Pete was an illusion that captured me hook, line, and sinker. The streets of St. Pete were so gutter that in order for you to survive on them you had to be a good fighter and be able to pull the trigger. The fact that I didn't have any trouble with either was a testament to my blind loyalty to those streets that cared nothing about me. I thought I was chasing fame and a name, but in reality, all I was chasing was a bunk in prison or a plot in the graveyard. In hindsight, I see myself rebelling against the system because, even as a grown man, I was still that little boy with no positive outlet in my life.

I was a true product of my environment. I was in love with the streets. As a teenager and into adulthood I was in love with the fast money and the even faster women that the streets offered. I was under the impression that I had it all, that I was on top. In reality, I was a big fool. Now that I sit here in these blues, these state-issued clothes, I reflect on my life and wish I had listened to my mother. It was hard for her to raise a man, but I should have let her.

So, in 1986, at the age of twenty, I was officially introduced to my blues. I guess I can say that I was blessed to be issued blues instead of a plot. Even with my first trip to prison, I didn't learn my lesson. Unfortunately, it took me four more trips to prison for me to understand that there's more to life than prison blues. This understanding wasn't immediate, because being sentenced to life and, at the time, being uneducated, I felt, "What's the use?"

The answer to that question came years later when I woke up one day and decided I wanted to change my life. I started by asking questions about the law, and in that process I was introduced to the GED instructor whose class I requested to be in. Before this I had no interest in doing anything constructive because I had fallen into the so-called "prison life." Anything that I could do wrong, I did. I was the classic case of letting my blues define who I was. But now I have a dream of one day soon becoming a paralegal. I know that if I learn the law, then I can become physically free of these blues. I'm already mentally free.

When I transferred to Tomoka Correctional Institution, I needed to involve myself in positive things, so I signed up for the Horizon Program, which is a faith and character-based program. I also enrolled in Community Education Project (CEP) provided by Stetson University. These two programs are driving me now. I've become a positive, caring person that's not just wearing blues, but thriving in them. I'm a fifty-three-year-old incarcerated man that's holding down a C average in CEP, and that's something I'm extremely proud of.

Now, I let the man that once lived in the stigma of a man in blues, a man unworthy of help or of another chance to get it right, be a man that just so happens to wear clothes the color of blue. I'm a living testament that a man can change if he really wants to. These blues that I wear don't define me. I define me. The choices and decisions that I make today will give me a brighter tomorrow. That's what I strive for. That's what makes me more than my blues.